ACCIDENTAL
RICH BOY

First published in the UK by Beacon Books and Media Ltd
Innospace, Chester Street, Manchester M1 5GD, UK.
Copyright © Akmal Ullah 2019

www.beaconbooks.net

Cataloging-in-Publication record for this book is available from the
British Library

Paperback ISBN 978-1-912356-27-0
Ebook ISBN 978-1-912356-28-7

Cover design by Moimoi.

ACCIDENTAL RICH BOY

Akmal Ullah

BEACON BOOKS

Acknowledgements

All praises and thanks are due onto God, for blessing me with the ability to write creatively and share it with the world.

I also want to thank my mother, who pushed and encouraged me to pursue excellence through education; my late father, who taught me how to be persistent and persevere through any hardship in the short time that I had him in my life; my wife, who pushed me to continue writing and yelled out different ideas each time I hit a 'brick wall'; my two beautiful children, who always made me laugh irrespective of how stressed I was whilst juggling work, family and writing; my two colleagues, James Mansfield and Naheeda Mizan who read my manuscript at different stages and provided me with helpful feedback; every student who I've ever had the pleasure of teaching, whose lives have always inspired me and fuelled my creativity; my close friends (you know who you are), who have always been at my side; my editor, Siema Rafiq, for the countless times she read my manuscript and helped me develop, refine and shape it; and finally, a huge thank you to Jamil Chishti at Beacon Books for allowing me to share my story.

Contents

Acknowledgements.......................................iv

1   The First Strike 1
2   The Cycle of Rags to Riches 7
3   Shelter...19
4   Home 'Sweet' Home............................27
5   The Main Strike 35
6   Banks...41
7   The Red Letter Day 55
8   The Man of the House 65
9   Street Boys...73
10   My Escape...79
11   The Visits...91
12   New Hope?...99
13   Money Talks 107
14   Mopeds...113
15   Just What I Needed 121
16   Mission Possible.............................127
17   Cell 6...133
18   Life on Bail...141
19   It Wasn't Me! 157
20   The Time Had Come 163
21   The Return 171
22   New Horizons.............................179

Glossary of Arabic Terms.............................183

Chapter 1

The First Strike

I was twelve years old when the first calamity struck in my life—or at least that's the first time I remember facing any real difficulty. A series of events took place in my life leading to what became an impossible situation and where I felt I had no choice but to do what I did. I know some people will judge me for the decisions I took, but let me take you back to the beginning, before the day everything changed, so you can understand how I ended up in this situation.

Even though we weren't rich, Mum and Dad always made sure that we had more than enough. We grew up on the Atlantic Estate, a council estate like many others in London, made up of endless rows of dull, lifeless concrete blocks. It wasn't the nicest place to live, but we didn't have much to complain about. Our parents gave us pocket money at the beginning of each week, filled us up with tasty treats at dinner time and bought us the latest Nike Air trainers at the end of each term so we could show them off to our friends at school.

Dad worked in a totally different part of London called Aldgate as a chef at The Cinnamon Club, which was part of a huge multi-national chain of hotels and restaurants. He let me tag along with him now and then, and wow, was it a place of luxury! It was clearly a place reserved only for the rich and wealthy. The tables were decorated with fancy tablecloths, carefully folded up napkins and fresh flowers. The waiters all wore white gloves and very smart clothes and there were at least five different types of cutlery pieces per person. Why would one person need all of those spoons, forks and knives? I wondered. It was all very unnecessary if you were just going out to eat.

Dad told us of Arab sheikhs reserving tables for £1,000 per night and people eating eight-course meals (the cheapest three-course meal was around £100, excluding drinks!) How is it possible to eat an eight-course meal? Surely you'd be stuffed by the time you got to course number three! But Dad told me they gave you very small portions of everything so you kept on ordering more food. How very clever, I thought, but why didn't people understand that the dishes were so small to keep you spending lots of money? Maybe it was the name and prestige of The Cinnamon Club that made people want to dine there, or maybe it was the quality of the food that made them willing to spend so much. Each time I went, I would see men dressed in black velvet penguin-tail dinner jackets and women wearing evening dresses with incredibly high-heeled shoes, flashing their expensive jewellery as the white-gloved waiters dashed around, bringing an endless supply of food and champagne to their tables.

Apart from the fact that it was a tall building, The Cinnamon Club couldn't have been more different to where we lived on the Atlantic Estate. Its sharp tip pierced the night sky like a spear, cutting through its surroundings, and the shiny, glass plates reflected inwards to create the effect of a precious stone, similar to the huge skyscrapers of Canary Wharf that I could see in the distance from my bedroom window. Towering over the skyline, they looked like sparkling giants looking down on the rest of us regular people living in high-rise buildings. Our homes were also home to many other families, with the entire block made up of twenty floors of mostly one and two bedroom flats. It was in a state of complete disrepair and the residents complained about just about everything: water leaks, lack of heating, damaged smoke alarms and infestations of mice and insects. The two lifts were always out of order (which was a pain if you lived on the top floor), but the council's repair number was always busy so people just gave up on contacting them. There were rumours of a huge 'refurbishment' and talks of 'regenerating' the local area, but the only change we saw was the creation of new buildings that kept mysteriously cropping up everywhere. It was strange to think that right next to the luxury flats lived people who could only dream of eating, drinking and living as their neighbours did.

Dad also told us of the fancy dress parties that took place at The Cinnamon Club over the Christmas holidays. That was always a busy period for Dad and he usually got home at three or four in the morning. We always knew that they'd had a party the previous night because he'd bring home different props: clown hats, fake moustaches, fake glasses with big noses attached to them, different types of masks and other weird looking items that I couldn't imagine anybody wearing, let alone people who were so posh.

The Cinnamon Club also had a casino attached to it. I wasn't allowed to go there when I visited with Dad because I wasn't old enough, but I always walked past and took a glimpse. I saw people walking around with gambling chips in their hands, others sitting around tables with roulettes, and some with cards in their hands, looking very tense like they were having trouble going to the toilet. There was also a long row of slot machines where I saw people inserting one pound coins and yanking the lever downwards, waiting for the machine to miraculously spit out loads of pound coins—that never happened, of course! The mixture of bright lights dazzled my eyes as I walked past the transparent glass walls of the casino like a child in a circus fair.

The strangest thing I saw there once was a man sitting in the middle of the nicely carpeted floor. He just sat there quietly and stared into space. Nobody even noticed him—they were too busy gambling their money away on the various colourful machines and tables, waiting eagerly to be handed their winnings. The security men quickly escorted him out. He didn't resist. They quite literally lifted him off the ground and took him outside. I stood watching for a few seconds, wondering why that man was just sitting there before Dad grabbed my hand and pulled me away.

"Come on, Nadim, we have to go," he said, tugging at my arm like I was a small child mesmerised in a toy shop. He must have lost a lot of money that night, I thought. That's probably why he was sitting there looking like he was paralysed. Maybe that's what gambling did to people when they lost. Maybe that's one of the reasons why it's so wrong.

"Don't stare at those big machines, Nadim. They eventually drain the life out of anyone who goes near them. You have to work hard and earn your money in this life. It won't fall into your lap by playing those stupid machines and hoping to become rich by chance."

That was Dad—always full of words of wisdom and life advice. I heard his voice inside my head every time I thought about that night. My fondest memory of him was when I was admitted to hospital at the age of eight because of my severe asthma. I was brought in by ambulance after suffering an asthma attack and the doctors did some tests on me to find the right medication to sort out my breathing. I was playing with cold water a few days earlier and became very unwell: first came the temperature, then the cold, which stirred up the asthma. Mum came in the mornings with breakfast and lunch after she dropped off my elder brother, Nabil, to school. She knew I hated hospital food and made every effort to bring me something different each day. Dad would arrive in the evenings and bring me dinner (he arranged to finish work slightly early when I was in hospital). Every evening I would eagerly await my meal—the best part about being in hospital was that Dad always cooked my favourite foods. He usually brought me roast chicken, tandoori chicken or Mexican chicken (yes, I loved chicken). One evening, I was really hungry and salivating at the thought of devouring a succulent chicken dish.

"Dad," I protested, giving him a devastated look of shock and horror after I opened the plastic heat-proof food container, "it's fish!" I had waited for hours for something decent to eat and he had brought me fish! He knew I hated fish and the only thing I ate was chicken, but he still brought me fish! The strong stench and oily texture from its glistening skin disgusted me. "I can't eat this. I hate fish. You know that." I crossed my arms over

5

my chest and gave Dad a deathly stare before deciding that I wasn't going to eat that evening. I'd just go to sleep.

"Listen, Nadim," he said, tilting my chin up with his hands. He let go, ran his fingers through his neatly brushed black hair and began to massage his temples with both hands. I could tell he was trying not to get frustrated. He let out a small sigh. "Why don't you just open the container properly and have a look?" I re-opened the container. The oily pieces with scaly skin still weren't appealing to me.

"Right, now take the container up to your nose and smell it," he insisted. A rich aroma shot up my nose and tickled my senses. What was happening? I thought to myself. Fish has never been able to do this to me before.

"That, my son, is no regular fish. It's a very expensive fish that we imported from Italy for a customer who requested it for his anniversary meal. It's quite rare and very tasty! Once you try it, you won't hate fish anymore. Just try it," he added, "it's not like anything you've ever had before, I promise!"

I reluctantly picked up my fork and ripped off a small bit of the fish. The taste was indescribable! A mixture of different flavours and spices ran along my tongue and the soft, tender pieces melted in my mouth as I gulped each piece down like a hungry monster. It was true—it wasn't like anything I'd tasted before and I never tasted fish like that again.

"You see, son, life is constantly changing and you have to be willing to adapt. Nothing stays the same. You have to be brave and try new things—sometimes things you've never tried before. That's how you stay on top of this ever-changing world."

Chapter 2

The Cycle of Rags to Riches

Dad was a very absent dad. Like many hardworking migrant dads, he worked almost all hours of the day and night. He left for work before we woke up to go to school and came back when we were asleep. He even worked on his days off and never took leave—he just took the extra money instead. All of this so we could live a life of luxury? No, not for us. Like many of his generation, he had it in his head that Britain only allowed people like him to enter the country to make up some sort of short-fall in certain employment areas and when they achieved what they wanted, the workers would all be sent back to their native countries. So for him, his time was limited. He wanted to work as hard as he could, save as much money as he could, build an empire 'back home' and then live a comfortable life there when the Brits sent him back. I don't think he ever dreamed that his children would grow up to become proud citizens of what he described as the 'host nation'. Our time in the UK never did expire (and I hope it never will). We comfortably identified as 'British' and 'Muslim', and to try to separate the two would be as painful as asking me who I loved more—my mum or my dad.

Anything that threatened our home had the power to unsettle me. Dad worked incredibly hard to buy the three-bedroom council flat that we lived in. It was the only thing he had to show for his day and night working pattern. He felt very fortunate that he could own his own home after living in temporary accommodation for so many years. Mum and Dad previously had to declare themselves homeless because the landlord they were renting from suddenly wanted to sell up. So they found themselves with nowhere to live and no deposit to secure another place. They could have gone to Mum's family and asked them for help, but Dad was much too proud to admit he was in trouble and ask for 'handouts'. When they finally did get a permanent council property, they were over the moon. Dad wanted to make that flat his castle and so, when he felt he could afford it and the council offered to sell it to him with a discount, he didn't let the opportunity slide away. He didn't care about how it looked or where it was.

Our tower block sat fiercely in the middle of the Atlantic Estate. The constant noises from the other flats meant you could never feel a sense of peace and quiet. The enormous size of the towers blocked out the sunlight, and the narrow alleyways and poorly maintained boiler rooms in the basement provided the perfect cover for youngsters to get up to mischief. Surrounded by other murky, harsh and dominating high-rise blocks, it also had a particular smell—a strange combination of smells created by the residents cooking different cuisines, urine and spilled alcohol bottles left over by the people that smoked and drank on the staircases at night. But none of that seemed to bother Dad. As long as we were comfortable inside, he didn't care about what happened on the outside. It was still home!

Most of the youngsters on the Atlantic Estate seemed to belong to another world. In the evening as the sun dipped, dark clouds gathered in the sky, giving birth to a new world. Looking out through my bedroom window, I could see and hear the 'street boys' at work. Loud hip-hop music blaring out swear words, piercing the air. The screech of burning rubber as the flashy cars roared their way in and out of the estate. Smoke flying out of the cars and hanging thick, poisoning the air. I often wondered who those dark figures were, and what it would be like to be one of them, or even know one of them. After the Ocean Youth Club closed down, there wasn't much to do on the estate. Instead, there seemed to be fights and rumours of fights almost every day—feuds that could easily lead to bloodshed even over the smallest of issues.

There were also, however, some decent people that lived on the Atlantic who came from families that tried to protect their children from that world. One such person was Musa, my next door neighbour. Musa's family had lived on the estate for over twenty years. His family arrived from Tangier in Morocco before I was born, and they were one of the first families to be housed in our tower. His dad described it as a 'palace' compared to the horrible places they'd lived in previously. Our families got on really well most of the time, but they did have their fair share of arguments. On one occasion it was because they left large bin bags outside of their front door and Mum found it difficult to navigate her double pushchair around the huge, overfilled, smelly black bin bags. The bin chutes were always blocked and most people couldn't be bothered to carry their rubbish all the way downstairs into the 'big bin house'. Mum and Dad were at breaking point when flies began to buzz around the rotting garbage and the smell started to slowly creep into our home. After several polite requests, Dad had a full blown argument with Musa's dad, which would have ended in a fist fight if Mum hadn't pulled him back. Our families stopped talking for ages after that and only made up when the holy month of Ramadan came around. Our mums always made an effort to break the tension by bringing over food for each other. Mum cooked her pilau rice with extra ghee and tandoori chicken for them, and they returned the gesture by bringing us some lamb tagine and handmade Moroccan sweets.

He was a lot older than me, but when Musa was younger he got himself mixed up with the street boys. He was physically bigger than most of them so they must have used him as their 'muscle', I guess. I remember seeing him outside every time I looked out of the window or when we went shopping with Mum. He was always out in a dark hoodie, passing things to the other boys and collecting money. I remember him once running up the communal stairs of our block to get home, a bandanna covering his face, blood on his light grey top and his right hand behind his back, hiding his knuckle dusters. That was the last I saw of him before he disappeared. He got kicked out of school early and ended up in prison by the time he was seventeen. When he came out, he was totally different. He grew a small beard, wore a prayer cap and spent most of his spare time either at the mosque attending the prayers, or volunteering at our local food bank. He worked as a postman, so I saw him on my way to school every morning. By that time all of his siblings had moved out of the family home, but he stayed on to look after his parents.

I sometimes felt lost for words when he shook hands with me and asked me how things were going. I'd always looked up to him in awe, not only because he seemed like a really cool, confident guy, but also because of the way he put his past behind him and stayed on the straight and narrow, despite the huge temptations that surrounded us on a daily basis.

* * *

Dad didn't come from a particularly religious family—it was Mum who helped cultivate love, hope and fear of Allah within us. Most of her family took religion quite seriously. They weren't boring and awkward—they just had a strong belief that as Muslims we should be proud of our faith and willing to mould our lives around the obligations and requirements of Islam.

She was the one who decided to pay a tutor, Ustaadh Akram, to teach us Qur'an, Arabic and prayers. Since Dad was absent, she thought it best we had a strong male figure to make us work hard. He came every Saturday morning and always greeted us with his soft voice and pleasant smile. Within the first few months, Nabil and I were able to read Arabic fluently (although we didn't understand everything yet), and we learnt how to offer our five daily prayers and various other supplications for the morning and evening. Dad would sometimes join us on Saturday mornings. I remember him once telling Ustaadh Akram how much he regretted not being able to recite the Qur'an often and how he felt guilty about rushing his prayers because work was so busy.

Not long after this, I noticed that Dad's work pattern changed. He'd come home a lot earlier than usual and even took a few days off here and there. He never seemed to be able to sit still when he was at home. Instead of slumping down on the sofa in front of the TV like we did, he'd pace around the flat, help Mum in the kitchen or go out to the mosque. Maybe he was trying to focus less on work and devote his time to other important things, like Islam and family, I thought. Until one day, Nabil and I woke up to the sound of Mum and Dad's loud, muffled voices.

"What's all that noise?" asked Nabil, still yawning and rubbing his eyes.

"I don't know, but it doesn't sound right," I replied, suddenly sitting upright in my bed.

Nabil tiptoed across the room and opened our bedroom door slowly. He leaned his right ear into the open gap to listen.

"What is it? What are they shouting about so early in the morning?"

Mum and Dad did have disagreements, but not like this. It was very unusual for them to be yelling so early in the morning.

"I can't hear much... their door's closed." Nabil shrugged and yawned again, before walking back and collapsing onto his bed. I sighed and decided to pretend that I was going to the toilet, which was past Mum and Dad's bedroom. I trod gently, trying to stop the floorboards from creaking under the carpet. I stopped at their door for a brief moment. I couldn't hear much. All I could hear was Mum crying, breathing heavily and repeating "They stole from us", "They took everything" and "They stole our children's future". I tried to listen in, but I still couldn't hear much. Resting my hand on the door frame, I leaned my ear close to their door. I know I shouldn't have, but I was desperate to know what was happening. My heart was pounding and my palms began to feel clammy as I heard Dad's footsteps pacing around his room. Who were 'they'? And what did they take? My mind raced, trying to find answers. They stopped speaking suddenly for a moment. The wind had blown the bathroom door right open. I spun around quickly, trying to stroll into the bathroom as casually as I could before they discovered me.

For most of that week, Dad was awake before we left for school and was at home by the time we got back—that wasn't right and he wasn't himself. He was very quiet and withdrawn. Mum was also very quiet and kept herself busy with the household chores. When it was time to eat, Mum left his food on the small table in the living room and went off to her room to pray and recite the Qur'an. For a while I couldn't put my finger on what was happening. I tried to read Mum and Dad's face, but they didn't give much away. The tense atmosphere didn't get any better either.

The arguments became more frequent. I heard them yelling at each other almost every day. They tried not to argue in front of us and took it to their bedroom or the kitchen, but at other times they got lost in their emotions and couldn't help but shout in front of us. I couldn't stand it when they argued like that. My throat dried up and my stomach would tie up in knots, to the point that even when Mum made my favourite tandoori chicken, I couldn't bring myself to eat it. I constantly bit my lips and gnawed on the inside of my cheeks, not even realising I was doing it until I tasted blood on my tongue. It soon became very obvious what they were arguing about. After two decades of paying the mortgage and 32 years of 'hard graft' and sacrifice, Dad had been made redundant. I can't ever remember Dad crying, except for that one time I was in hospital with severe asthma. But when he suddenly found himself at home without a routine, he cried. Not out loud and not in front of anybody, but I could hear quiet whimpers when walking past his room. I often caught him wiping his tears away when we were around.

Mum was furious with Dad. Not about the redundancy—that came all of a sudden—but because of all the money that he sent overseas to build his 'empire' in Bangladesh. He trusted his brothers to invest it for him. Only they didn't. They wasted most of it on whatever suited them and the small amount of land and property they did buy, they bought it under everyone's name so Dad had no way of selling it and getting any money.

"Your family robbed us!" she screamed. Her fair skin glowed red like the tip of a flame. She sat down with her hands over her face. Until now I'd never witnessed that small, petite figure that was my mum muster so much rage—she was really upset. "I didn't mind you building a house for them, paying for their upkeep or building tube wells so everyone in the local village could have clean water, but why did you keep sending money for them to buy land? I'm not craving to live like the rich and wealthy— you know I didn't marry you for that, but your family stole our future! Why did you trust them with absolutely everything?" I watched as she wiped her tears and ran her fingers through her untied, thick black hair before dropping her head down and gazing mindlessly at the floor.

"They're my family," he replied quietly, shaking his head, "my own flesh and blood. I never expected my own brothers to squander my hard-earned money."

"But why did you send them absolutely every penny?" she pressed further, fighting back tears. "Why didn't you leave some money here for us, for a rainy day?"

"I don't know," he mumbled, his voice muffled by the hands that covered his face. "I shouldn't have trusted them so blindly. I should have kept an eye on them."

Dad had his own way of dealing with Mum and it wasn't arguing back because he knew she was right. He walked out, finished his entire twenty pack of cigarettes (even though he knew how bad it was for his health) and then came back a few hours later. Mum prepared his dinner and left it on the kitchen table. They didn't speak to each other until the next day.

Out of my three siblings, for some reason I felt that I was the only one who really understood what was happening. That's probably why it affected me so much. Nabil, although older than me, didn't care too much.

"Chill, man, the council will take care of it," he said, not looking up from his phone. "Stop worrying, bruv."

He was 15 years old and more interested in making sure he had the latest trainers and hanging out with his mates than about the fact that we might lose the roof over our heads. And my two younger twin sisters, Nabeela and Nusaybah, were only four years old so I didn't expect them to understand anything, although they must have been affected by the constant arguing.

Things got so bad between them that I genuinely thought Mum would just 'pack it in' and leave. I couldn't bring myself to think about them breaking up. What would happen to us if Mum and Dad ever separated? The mere thought of it ripped me up inside. But she didn't leave. I guess she couldn't. Mum loved Dad, even though she was really angry with him for making stupid decisions. Being the eldest in the family, Dad felt responsible for his family back home. He was dutiful to his parents and took care of everyone by sending money every month. Mum never stopped him from doing so—in fact, she encouraged him because she knew how important it is to look after your parents. She just didn't like the fact that Dad blindly trusted his brothers with everything.

I didn't know what to think and feel. My heart tugged at me, feeling torn between two of the most important people to me in the world. Mum was only furious at Dad because she was very protective of us and didn't want us to face any hardships, but how was Dad supposed to know his family, his own flesh and blood, would rip him off and leave him with nothing? I couldn't help but feel that he was a victim too.

* * *

The letter sat on the kitchen table for a few days. NOTICE FOR SEEKING POSSESSION written in bright red capital letters so you couldn't mistake it for anything else and sent via registered post so you couldn't claim you didn't receive it.

How did this come about? It's simpler than you might think. Dad's redundancy was in the process for over eight weeks. As usual, he thought he could handle it. His plan was to ask his brothers to sell some investments from 'back home'. He planned to live off that until his agreed severance pay came through. He would live off that money and pay off the rest of the mortgage and then retire early. Except things never go to plan and they certainly didn't for him. We always plan, but Allah, from His Infinite Wisdom, sometimes has a different plan for us. The difficulty is being able to have full trust in that plan. The ultimate test of faith is to have trust in Allah and 'let go'—something I've always found difficult to do because I always want to be in control of things. It took me a long time to realise that I didn't have control over everything.

The severance pay had to go through the company processes, which sometimes took up to four months. In the meantime, there was no chance of getting any money from his investments and as a family we weren't entitled to any state benefits because Dad was still classified as 'employed' with overseas assets (even though he couldn't access them).

So for a period of time, there was little money at home. Mum and Dad had enough in their bank accounts to pay for the food for a month, but no money to cover the bills and mortgage. For twenty-one years dad paid into that mortgage, but even then there was about £22,000 of the debt still remaining and the bank wouldn't write that off! The system doesn't work like that. Banks don't have emotions. They just deal with you like another number, never understanding that there are real people—men, women and children—behind every statistic.

So, within four weeks of missing a payment, that horrid letter arrived. It threatened us with eviction along with the FINAL DEMAND notices from the gas, electricity, water and phone companies, always written in blood-red capital letters, making you feel that the words were staring at you accusingly.

When I thought about all of that and contemplated what could happen if we lost our home, it felt like I had the entire world's troubles on my shoulders. After the *isha* prayers, each night as I lay in bed, I didn't sleep—I couldn't! My body was tired but my brain kept working overtime. I tossed and turned, fighting with my brain to shut it down and let me sleep. When I finally did fall asleep, I had the most disturbing nightmares. I saw myself outside our tower block trying to enter the communal door at the entrance. I used my fob key over and over again and tugged at the handle desperately, but it refused to open. I looked up to the second floor and saw our balcony, but my heart sank as I realised that I couldn't reach it. Tired, annoyed and shedding tears, I looked up to the sky and the dark clouds raced towards me, smashing everything in its path before hitting me in the face.

Chapter 3

Shelter

Tyler and Chantal lived on the ground floor beneath us in a small two-bedroom flat, which had damp problems and a very flimsy front door. The ground floor flats didn't have the extra security of a main fob key entry door like all the other residents on our tower did, which being in an area like ours was very important, especially with the street boys creeping out of every corner of the estate as soon as daylight disappeared. Even though our lifts stank of urine and alcohol and were plastered with graffiti and swear words, the solid heavy steel door of the main entrance provided an extra sense of safety and security.

Tyler and Chantal both went to my school and my family really got on with theirs. Tyler's mum sometimes asked me to do the shopping for her when she couldn't go out as she'd just had a baby. She always said thank you and even paid me £2.50, which I spent buying sweets for everyone.

Tyler's mum and dad rented from a private landlord after waiting for years on the council waiting list, but with the arrival of a new baby, they were overcrowded once again. This time Tyler's dad managed to get their housing application reactivated so they were on the official waiting list, bidding for homes every week (although

Tyler's mum told us that they were at the bottom of the list and the average waiting time for a family home was about ten years).

They soon fell into difficulty when Tyler's dad suddenly lost his job as a construction worker. Even though they were on full benefits, the cuts meant that they found it really difficult. Within two months, Tyler's parents found themselves in rent arrears of about £2,000 which they had no way of paying. Their landlord wasn't understanding and applied to the courts to evict them.

Tyler's mum was a very friendly, larger than life character. She was loud and boisterous and you could always hear when she argued with her husband even though we were two floors above them. She was also very strict with Tyler and Chantal. But to us, she was just a jolly, bubbly woman who had a sense of humour and tried to force feed us if we ever visited their flat. Mum and I visited often. She tried to keep the place clean and tidy, but the smell of burnt cooking oil and sticky sweat always wafted up my nose. The carpet was covered in black patches and cigarette burns and there were dark green spots on the walls where the damp was rising. I always noticed the sticky mouse traps that had been neatly wedged in the corners of the room.

Tyler often needed my help with his History and English homework, which is what we did whilst our mums got on with their 'mum chats' over tea and biscuits. But when we visited Tyler's mum leading up to that horrible Saturday morning, she looked visibly shaken and scared. She wasn't her usual self—no jokes, no tea and juice, and definitely no handmade fairy cakes.

"I don't know what I'm gonna do, love," she told Mum, trying to hold back her tears. "This is our home. We've spent so much money buying furniture and decorating it and now the landlord wants to take it back! Where are we gonna go? I've tried speaking to the Housing Benefits department, but they just won't increase the payments. The cuts are apparently government policy!" She began to sob profusely.

"Have you tried going to the Citizens Advice Bureau?" asked Mum, fishing out a tissue from her handbag.

"Well, they said the council should be able to help me cos of the kids, but they won't step in until we've actually been evicted. So we've literally gotta be on the streets before they put us in a B&B! How does that make any sense?" she cried.

"I know it doesn't. Just try to remain strong." Mum placed her hand on Brenda's shoulder.

"I'm really trying to... it's just the kids! I feel like I've let them down! Don't know what to do," she whimpered, wiping her tears and taking a deep breath.

"Just hold tight, Brenda. We're all here for you. When you get the official eviction letter, I'll come to the council with you myself and we'll get everything sorted!"

They lived in fear for about four weeks, until suddenly, early one Saturday morning, their fears became reality. A big, dark van pulled up outside our tower block. I watched from our balcony as two formally dressed men with body-cams emerged from the vehicle. Both of them looked around as though they were searching for something. I saw one pointing whilst the other made a hand gesture towards the back. Their mouths moved as they spoke, but I couldn't hear what they were saying. One of the men pulled out a piece of paper, fluttering against the wind. Finally, they knocked on the door. A pause. A moment of calm, right before the storm. I hurried downstairs to get closer.

"What do you want me to do?" Tyler's dad yelled. "Where do you want me to go? I've got small children. How are we supposed to survive on the streets?" He was shouting at the top of his voice, saliva spraying out of his mouth. His face was red with rage and his blonde hair, usually tied in a neat ponytail, hung out and bounced with every shout. He clenched his fists and breathed heavily, like he was about to completely lose control.

By this point almost everyone had heard the commotion and a small crowd of neighbours had gathered outside their flat. Mum also came rushing down to help Tyler's mum but she couldn't get through.

The two men called the police. When they arrived, they forced their way through the crowd of onlookers, carving a pathway through a dense forest. Things seemed to calm down as the police officers tried to break the stalemate between the two men and Tyler's dad, who was blocking their way into the flat. I saw Musa observing the scene with a confused look on his face.

"I'm sorry we have to do this, sir, but we're just doing our job," the older of the two men said in a calm and measured tone. "We are High Court enforcement officers. I know this must be a difficult time for you but I'm afraid we have a High Court writ that we need to enforce. You are in rent arrears and your landlord has applied to the courts to have you evicted."

The mild-mannered approach had no effect on Tyler's dad—in fact, it seemed to make him even more furious.

He said he couldn't believe that neither the courts nor the landlord had given him notice that an eviction order was granted and that he and his family had to vacate the property. He knew it was in the process, but looked like he had been thrown completely caught off-guard by the shockingly fast rate at which it all happened. He didn't have time to plan, prepare or fight against it. He told the enforcement officers that he had no idea that the matter had progressed to court as he was given the Notice to Seek Possession by the estate agent only last month.

"Where am I supposed to go?" he kept repeating. "The Housing Office is closed over the weekend. Where am I supposed to put my kids?" After nearly an hour of arguing, Tyler's mum came out and tried to calm her distressed husband.

"It's no use, love," she cried, wiping her tears with her T-shirt. "They've got a court order."

"But what are we supposed to do with the kids?" he asked through gritted teeth.

The enforcement officers gave the family only two hours to grab their essentials and vacate the flat. They quickly began to change the locks. It was obvious they'd done this before.

In his white, short-sleeved *thobe* draped over his blue Adidas tracksuit bottoms, Musa's towering, muscular figure stood out from the crowd as he leapt into action like a giant bear, trying to control the restlessness whilst making phone calls to the Housing Office emergency number and social services. He even called our local primary school in a desperate attempt to try and help the family secure some sort of accommodation at least until Tuesday when they would have to go to the Housing Office and declare themselves 'homeless'. But it was no use. It was the Saturday morning before a long bank holiday weekend and nobody answered their phones.

Tyler's family slowly packed their bags with all the essentials they needed for the weekend and tried to empty out the flat as much as they could. Tyler's uncle came around with his white van and offered to take them in for the weekend. He worked as a builder and luckily lived nearby. He was the only person that could help them in that very dire situation. He filled up his van with the belongings they brought out—some were in black bin bags, others in rucksacks, but a lot of things, like the children's toys, were left trailing behind on the floor.

The enforcement officers handed Tyler's dad some paperwork to take with him when he visited the Housing Office on Tuesday. "Here is a copy of the eviction order. Please show it to the Housing Office and your social worker, which they will assign to you. You have children so this document should give you some priority with the housing people," he explained. "Here is my number. You can call me directly to come and pick up the rest of your stuff when you're ready. Good luck."

I saw the landlord sitting in his car a few metres away from the crowd, watching the whole situation unfold in front of his eyes. As the enforcement officers handed him the new keys to the flat, he did nothing to help or support the distressed family. But why would he? He was clearly in this business for the money—he didn't care about anything else!

By now the whole family and their belongings had been squeezed into the van. Tyler's dad jumped into the front with his brother, and wiping his tears with what looked like a dishcloth, was driven away into the distance.

* * *

What happened to Tyler's family played on my mind all day. I couldn't believe that all those memories and the place they once called home had been ripped away from them so heartlessly.

Later that evening, I took those colourless, washed-out stairs down to Tyler and Chantal's flat. I hated taking the stairs, but the lifts were out of order—again. The stench of the rough sleepers from the previous night was overpowering despite the strong disinfectant the cleaners had used. The floor glistened wet, drying slowly. I knew I couldn't go inside, but I just wanted to take another look at the flat. The place was boarded up with brass-coloured metal frames like a cage. I felt a mixture of hurt and disgust. Hurt for what Tyler's family must be going through and disgust at the fact that people were being forced out into the harsh, cold city streets whilst flats remained empty, securely shut to prevent anyone else from going inside. I sat on the stairs beside what used to be their front door with my head in my hands, trying to make sense of how any of this was fair.

I had just witnessed my worst nightmare play out in real life. With our own eviction letter still sitting on the kitchen table, I couldn't help but think, it could happen to us! It could happen to anyone! As I stared at the flat, I felt everything around me freeze: the noisy children on the balconies above me, the hurried movements of the street boys, and the screaming wind as it swept through the tower. My heart felt as heavy as a rock in my chest, my stomach tied itself into knots like a rope and my mouth dried up like a cotton ball. I couldn't breathe. I was gasping for air. The sour taste in my mouth made me feel sick. I felt a stab of guilt because I still had a roof over my head whilst Tyler's family were out there in the wilderness of London, not knowing where they would be sleeping tomorrow. I could still hear them like they were still in there—inside the flat. The sound of Brenda's voice, loud and husky, Tyler and Chantal's uncontrollable laughter and the distressed cry of their new baby had been drilled in my mind. My ears strained for the sound of the door lock turning to invite me in. It wasn't fair! I tried to hold my tears back, but it didn't work. Hot and painful, they slid down my cheeks. I felt angry. I wanted to kick and punch the graffiti-stained wall and tear down the metal boards. I wished I hadn't seen them get dragged out of their home. I felt dirty, like I was somehow part of the process as I watched on, unable to do anything. All I could do was go home, make *wudu* and pray. The warm water would wash away the dread that I felt in my heart and the stain of what I had witnessed this morning.

Chapter 4

Home 'Sweet' Home

The familiar tower block that I called home stood looming over me like a giant creature. The decaying paving of the concrete floor at the main entrance rubbed against the soles of my shoes, making an eerie scratching sound. Summoning what little courage I could muster, I entered. The place was dead silent. I twisted the handle to open the familiar front door. It closed sternly behind me. The darkness enveloped me and the vilest stench assaulted my nostrils. It was the smell of death. It was so strong I could almost taste it. By this time, my heart was beating so fast I could feel the vibrations in the top of my throat. The fear, coupled with the darkness of the night, blinded me. As I walked on, my vision adjusted slowly, and a dirty, dishevelled figure began to form in front of me. I blinked. I couldn't believe my eyes. It was Dad! But not the usual smart, well-dressed and confident looking Dad I always knew. This one was pale, his beard overgrown and his hair unkempt. His clothes were dirty and torn, as though he'd been sleeping rough. As the figure edged closer, he began to look increasingly sinister. This can't be real, I told myself. I wanted to get out of there. I needed to.

I woke up bathed in my own sweat. My clothes were drenched but my throat was quite the opposite—as dry as a desert. I was gasping for air and water. Thank God it was just a nightmare, I thought, although reality wasn't much better. I had woken up from a terrible nightmare of the previous night to the grim nightmare of reality. Nothing had changed. I'd do anything not to be feeling this way, I thought. I'd give anything.

I spent weeks in a whirlwind state of worry. I went to school but in body only—my mind was busy thinking about the fragile situation at home. Although sometimes I wouldn't think of home at all. I often found myself drifting off in lessons, my mind conjuring up the wildest things. I thought about how cool it would be if I could fly, and I would imagine flying all over the world like superman—not saving or rescuing anyone, but simply flying, taking in all of the scenery below me. Then my mind moved on to the kick-boxing lessons Dad used to take me to when I was at primary school. I imagined myself exploding in a moment of rage when my Maths teacher demanded my attention, storming out of the classroom, punching everyone who stood in my way. I don't know why my mind kept conjuring up these imaginary situations, but I didn't mind. It was much better than thinking about home.

One afternoon after Mum picked us up from school, Dad burst into the living room. He was out of breath. His trembling hands held up a hastily-opened envelope and a letter imprinted with a symbol I recognised only too well: The Cinnamon Club's emblem.

"It's done," he exclaimed. "We're safe. The kids are safe! Our home is safe!" He fell into prostration. "*Alhamdulillah*, Allah has saved us. I was so scared, so scared for us. But we don't need to fear anymore."

He began to jump up and down. He couldn't contain himself. He was shaking and frantically kissed and hugged everyone one by one, ending with Mum, who was still sitting on the sofa. He kneeled down and held her, his head completely lost in her flowing, untied hair. He held her for what seemed like an overwhelmingly long time.

"What, love? What are you talking about? What's happened?" asked Mum, bewildered, trying to make sense of Dad's behaviour. Dad's face emerged, covered in tears. He stood upright, without saying a word. The air felt heavy with anticipation.

"It's... it's my severance pay," he said quietly. "It's here. It's finally come through! It should clear in the bank account first thing tomorrow morning. I've calculated it and it's not going to make us rich, but it's more than enough alhamdulillah! Enough not only to pay the overdue bills and mortgage, but to pay off the entire remaining mortgage debt! The flat will be ours and nobody can take it from us then."

Mum didn't say anything. She stood with her eyes transfixed for a moment, and then her mouth broke out in the most radiant smile. She stood up and threw her arms around Dad. She was a lot shorter than Dad so I found it funny when they stood close to each other. Dad was about six foot and average build, but Mum's small and dainty figure made him appear massive. She finally let out a cry. That was the first time I saw them hug in such a long time. I couldn't help but beam as I watched her disappear into his arms.

Dad also decided to retire early so his private pension came through, which meant that he got paid a salary even though he didn't work! He had worked for 32 years non-stop, so maybe now was the time to rest. He did odd jobs here and there in his friends' restaurants, but nothing like before.

We all started to see a lot more of Dad. He took us to school and picked us up and attended all the school assemblies and sports days. He even offered to be the stage director in our year group's production of Aladdin. He was also a lot closer to Mum, doing the things that you expect a husband to do like giving her a hand with the household chores, taking her out for dinner, buying her flowers on occasions (which she continued to water even several days after they had died), and remembering birthdays and anniversaries after many years of continuously missing them. Mum seemed a lot happier. As a family we did all the things I'd always dreamed of doing like a weekend away at Alton Towers, having picnics on the beach in Brighton and going out for meals when Pizza Hut did their buffets and free refillable drinks on Thursday nights. Those moments felt extra special and fun because we'd never been able to experience it before.

But it wasn't fun for long. All those years of non-stop work finally caught up with Dad. Two years after retiring, he became very unwell. No one knew how unwell he really was until our GP, Dr Frazer, called one afternoon and explained Dad's situation to us. He said he was surprised that Dad hadn't collapsed already and insisted that we bring him in immediately so they could carry out some tests. They had discovered some abnormalities in Dad's routine blood test and wanted to investigate further.

In the following months they made a care plan for Dad, which included medications, recommendations for lifestyle changes and regular appointments at the hospital cardiology department. Dad took the medication and attended the appointments, but never listened to any of the lifestyle changes that they recommended for him, which included changes he had to make to his diet. One thing Dad loved was food and he wasn't going to obey anyone who told him what he could and couldn't eat.

"If I'm going to die, I won't die starving. I'll see death well-fed, enjoying the dishes I love," he said. "I'll go on the brisk walks and do the light exercises. I'll even cut down on the smoking. But I am not going to give up lamb biryani, butter chicken, rogan josh and my roasts. That's not gonna happen!" He was as stubborn as an ox!

His first heart attack came only two months after the doctors warned him to make some serious lifestyle changes. It happened right outside our front door. Dad came home from the mosque after the Friday *jummu'ah* prayers. He was rushed to hospital and became unconscious in the ambulance on the way. We thought we had lost him. I remember seeing him on the hospital bed with various leads coming out of his body, attached to the monitors around him.

When he finally did come around, he looked visibly shaken. He knew something had changed. He was no longer the fit, strong man that could work eighteen-hour days with very little sleep. Now, he couldn't eat anything and had to be drip-fed through his nose. He looked very different. He became very thin and his naturally tanned complexion turned pale. His face looked like it had been sucked inwards, making his eye sockets and cheekbones more visible—a stark contrast to his usually full-looking face and raised, square-shaped jaw. His once finely pushed back hair was untidy and his well-groomed beard was now scruffy. He also had bags under his eyes and nervously bit his bottom lip every few seconds. Whenever we came to visit, he struggled with all of his strength to try and sit up straight on his hospital bed.

"I know why this is happening now," he whimpered. The wire in his nose gave him a slight gurgling sound when he spoke. "It's Allah's punishment for all those years that I neglected my Lord and focused on the *dunya*. Look at me! I'm being denied food because I was careless and didn't take care of my body. Maybe Allah is punishing me for all those fasts that I found so difficult to keep when I was cooking in the Cinnamon kitchen. I know I tried to make up the fasts, but I could never really remember how many I missed."

"Don't be silly," snapped Mum. "We have a Lord who is Kind, Merciful and Forgiving. I know you made mistakes and neglectful, but Allah is Merciful. All you need to do is make sincere *tawba* and *istighfaar* and He will forgive you."

"I know," he nodded, swallowing hard. "I'm not complaining. I know how neglectful I was of Allah. I just hope He forgives me now that I've realised."

"He will. Just have good thoughts of Allah and expect good from Him." He lay back down and let out a distressed sigh, staring at the drip machine as it slowly poured the thick 'nourishing' liquid through his nose and into his body.

* * *

Mum spent most of her time with him beside his hospital bed. She went there early in the morning, taking the twins with her. They entertained themselves with toys

32

and puzzles and Mum took a collection of books to read while Dad rested. She tried to give Nabil the responsibility of helping out around the home, but she couldn't rely on him. Nabil never did as Mum asked. He spent most of the night out with his friends, which meant that Mum had to do everything. I saw the physical effects that all of it was having on her. She was travelling to and from the hospital every day, coming home to tidy and cook for us, as well as keeping up to date with all the bills and shopping. She wasn't eating or sleeping properly and was always agitated. I couldn't speak to her because she snapped even at the smallest of things. Sometimes I heard her crying at night when everyone was asleep.

We all slowly adapted when Dad came out of hospital. He finally did make some lifestyle changes. He quit smoking and gave up eating the oily, fatty things he loved so much. But it was too late. Within six months, he suffered another heart attack. This time I couldn't go to the hospital. I couldn't see him like that again. I was so used to seeing him as a strong, confident man who could take on the whole world. I stayed away because I hated hospitals, maybe because I spent so much time there myself when I had trouble with my asthma. Dad asked for me on several occasions. Each time, I made a different excuse about why I couldn't come. I think in the end he probably knew why.

When I finally did pluck up the courage to visit, Dad's health took a turn for the worse. Although they managed to revive him the first time he went into cardiac arrest, the doctors warned us that it could happen again and that we should start planning for Dad's eventual departure. They said that they didn't expect him to last more than 48 hours and that we should inform any friends and family who would like to see him for the final time. We knew we were going to lose him. The exact time, of course, was up to Allah.

Thankfully the doctors were wrong on that occasion and Dad soldiered on, until one dark night in November when his heart finally gave in.

Mum was in a complete state of despair and anguish that night. She cried for hours, sobbing really loudly with her face in her hands, wailing, "Why me? What did I do to deserve this?!"

I tried to take control of the situation. I sat next to her, took her hand and tried to comfort her, but I was breaking up inside. I swallowed hard, wrapping my arms around Mum as she burrowed her head in my chest. I wanted to cry, but I couldn't. Part of me just couldn't accept that it was true. How could it be? How could it be that one moment Dad was with us and the next he wasn't? I was numb. Too numb to speak, too numb to cry, too numb to think.

The next day Nabil and I went to the registry office to certify Dad's death and made the funeral arrangements. We prayed Dad's *janazah* and buried him on a Thursday straight after the *zuhr* prayers. At the burial site, Nabil and I went down inside the grave, carefully lowering Dad's body to his final resting place in the Gardens of Rest.

Chapter 5

The Main Strike

Dad's passing was a great loss because he wasn't just a family member—he was the 'glue' that stuck everyone together. When Dad died, we had to fend for ourselves again. We all missed him unbearably, although we all dealt with our grief in different ways. Mum was only 44 years old and feared how she would live out the rest of her life alone. The twins went very quiet for a while. I tried so hard to try to remember all of the good times we shared together because those were the memories I wanted to have and hold onto.

Nabil seemed to be the most affected out of all of us. He blamed himself for not being able to do anything when Dad fell ill and slowly got worse. It wasn't his fault. It was nobody's fault, I guess. But Nabil didn't see it that way. Grief does different things to different people.

I noticed that Nabil started acting very differently shortly after we buried Dad. He spent almost all of his time with the street boys now. In fact, I couldn't distinguish him from them anymore. The lack of sleep made his under eyes very puffy and his eyes looked watery like a glazed doughnut—they looked strained, like he was struggling to keep them open. When I looked in his eyes he didn't seem like Nabil, my annoying elder brother who I always bickered with. He was someone else and somewhere else, drifting further and further away from the world we lived in.

"I keep seeing him," he said, sitting on his bed with his knees pressed against his chest. He stared at the ground, his eyes fixed on a spot, fidgeting with his thumbs. "Night time is really bad," he continued with a blank stare. "I keep seeing Dad's body, covered in the white shroud we buried him in. I can't sleep."

"Bro, you need to tell someone. A doctor, maybe," I suggested, staring at his blank face. He looked lost, withdrawn.

"No, I don't need to," he snapped, jumping off from his bed. "Anyone who finds out will think I've gone mad."

"You're not mad, but I can see what all this is doing to you. You're not well, bro."

"I don't need anyone looking out for me," he said, trying to avoid eye contact. "I can take care of myself."

"But you can't! You can't take care of yourself! You have to stop hanging around with those idiots," I felt my voice rising to a shout. I just wanted him to listen. "They're just giving you that stuff to numb your mind, but it isn't good for you! We've already lost Dad. I don't want to lose you too."

He turned around, his face ugly with anger. "I didn't ask for your opinion. You deal with things your way and I'll deal with them my way. I'm not harming anyone but myself, so I don't need you sticking your nose in."

"Nabil," I pleaded, lowering my voice, trying to contain my frustration. "I'm really worried about you. Please, you have to stop this. Can't you see what's happening to you? You're out all hours of the night, you skive college, you mix with people you wouldn't even normally look at and now you've started a new habit—a bad habit that could eventually kill you."

"You haven't said anything to Mum, have you?" he asked, his eyes darting around the room.

"No I haven't, but she's not stupid," I whispered loudly, trying not to raise my voice. "She's bound to find out soon. Just look at the state of you."

"Look, I'll stop that stuff, okay? For now, I just need it to help me sleep." He lay down on his bed, closed his watery eyes and dozed off.

A few days later, he told me he dropped out of college.

"Nabil what's going on with you?" I asked him, trying not to sound patronising.

"Nothing, bro, nothing," he replied. His eyes were bloodshot red.

"You need to get back on the horse, do what you're good at."

"Like what, man?" he laughed sarcastically. "I ain't got the patience for college no more."

"So what are going to do with yourself? You were always good at school. I remember you saying how much you enjoyed Maths and Science after that parents' evening last year."

Nabil scoffed. "I was a kid then. I'm not that person anymore."

"So what now? What's your plan?"

"Maybe I'll get a job, make some money. What's the point of school? It's money everyone's after in the end anyway, right?" He looked at his reflection in the mirror on our bedroom wall and opened his eyes really wide, staring into them as if he was looking for something.

"Yeah but at least after a good education you'll get a good job and better money. Now you'll have to take whatever you get?"

"Yeah, right. There's a better way to make money without wasting your time in a classroom."

"What do you mean?" I couldn't help but get frustrated at him. "Don't do anything stupid, bro, please. 'Street life' isn't as easy as you think."

"Why not? Look at them lads on the estate. They work for themselves and don't have to answer to no boss. They drive nice cars, wear nice clothes..."

"Yes, and they're always looking over their shoulders. How many of them end up in jail or dead before they even reach twenty? Please, bro," I pleaded with him, "we don't need any more heartache in this family."

"Just leave me alone, man. You don't get it."

Eventually, he did see sense and got himself a job at our local supermarket, followed by another job at the Post Office, followed by another one at a grocery nearby. He went through three different jobs in the space of two months and could never hold one down. For one reason or another, he got sacked or just walked out. He was angry—angry at the world for everything!

"It's not fair, man. Life's not fair," he said, straight after he lost his job at the grocer's following an argument with one of the managers. "Why do bad things always happen to good people? What have I ever done? Why did Dad have to leave us like that after giving everything he had to his family back home?" His voice began to crack and I saw his eyes well up. He clenched his fists.

"Life's what you make it, bro. You'll find another job *inshallah*." I sat beside him, trying to comfort him.

An overpowering stench shot up my nostrils. "Have you been...?"

"Nothing, man. I ain't been doing nothing," he interrupted. He jumped up and punched the wardrobe with his right fist. "No more dead-end jobs and no more stupid managers thinking they can talk to me the way they want!" he yelled.

"Bro, calm down, things will work out inshallah. Please don't do anything stupid. We all need you."

He grabbed his jacket and stormed out of the flat. I didn't see him much after that. He got himself mixed up with one of the gangs on our estate, spending most of his days and nights out with them. One night, he didn't come home at all. Four days later, he appeared in front of a judge who sentenced him to two years in a young offenders' institution for aggravated burglary and drug dealing.

It all happened so quickly. Mum just seemed numb throughout the whole process. I guess losing Dad did that to her. I wished I had done more, but what could I have done? He was three years older than me and was so sure of himself, so confident and popular. The younger kids all wanted to be like him and everyone wanted to hang out with him. All of that attention must have got to his head. Dad's passing made him realise that he didn't have control over everything. I guess that's what broke him down. He used to have answers for everything (or at least he thought he did) and he was always so stress-free and laid-back. But then he saw Dad getting ill and weaker each day. That was hard for all of us but with him being the eldest, it must have affected him in ways that I can't imagine.

The next time I spoke to him was on his first day in prison after the sentencing. We didn't go to court—he told Mum he didn't want us there. He was ashamed of himself. He didn't even want us to visit him in prison, but Mum forced him to give us the details of where he was being held.

He called home. "Nadim, I'm so sorry, bro," his voice sounded muffled like he'd been crying. "I know I've let you all down. I swear I didn't do that stuff to get rich quick. I was just trying to get by. Still, I shouldn't have done it. I was so stupid! You're the man of the house now and I know you'll do a much better job than me. You'll be as good as Dad."

"Nabil," I said, trying to hold back my tears and prevent my voice from cracking up, "I told you. I told you about hanging around that lot. They're no good."

"It wasn't them," he interrupted. "It was me. It was all me. I blame myself. Mum and Dad tried to bring me up the right way, but I chose to make bad choices in life. It's my fault. Nobody else's!"

"How am I supposed to deal with things by myself?"

"You'll figure out a way," he said confidently. "You've always been the wise, cautious one in the family. Just stay strong and be there for Mum. I'll be back soon."

Chapter 6

Banks

With Dad having passed away and Nabil no longer home, life became really difficult. It felt like we were at a point of decline, receding like the water from a tide as it returns to sea. I was struggling to keep the family together. No matter what I did and no matter how much she tried to hide it, Mum was really unhappy. I was fifteen years old and it was the year of my GCSEs, but I felt like I had so many other things to worry about.

Our financial situation wasn't great. For some reason everything was just getting more and more expensive. People talked about a 'recession' happening and 'inflation' going up, but none of that made much sense to me and to be honest, I never really tried to understand it. We were just trying to survive, taking each day as it came. Mum tried to put on a brave face. She told us not to worry and reminded us that Allah is the best of providers.

She inherited Dad's pension, but she was only allowed half of it. That meant that we had to live on half of what we lived on when Dad was around, and Mum wasn't eligible for any state benefits because she had an 'income'. At least we didn't have to worry about the roof over our heads anymore. But as always, life brought about a new challenge, another thing to worry about and struggle through. This time it was putting food on the table, paying the bills, and trying to keep afloat.

I could tell Mum was struggling. The money wasn't enough. She thought about finding a job, but then who would look after us? A nanny would be too expensive—she would have to pay whatever she earned at her job towards childcare costs. It didn't make sense.

We ploughed through each day not knowing what the next day would bring, budgeting as carefully as we could. Mum taught us to make lots of *du'a* to Allah and ask Him to find us some relief from this difficulty. If only I could get a job. That would help. But at the age of fifteen, it's not even legal to work—it wasn't Dickens' London.

Mum struggled to pay for the weekly shopping, our lunch money, and still put money aside for the bills when they came every three months. Even though we no longer had a landline telephone or internet, she just about managed to pay the gas, water and electricity bills. Switching energy providers made little difference. There was talk about the government freezing energy prices for the next three years—as if the big, rich companies would allow that! Every time we got a bill, Mum was on the phone to the energy company telling them that there were fewer people living in the flat compared to a few years ago, so why had the bills increased so much?

"Mum, it's getting a bit embarrassing." I slumped onto the creaking sofa. "This is the third trip this term that I can't go to."

"There isn't much I can do, darling," she said, running her fingers through her greying hair, which draped loosely around her shoulders. "I'm running a tight ship. Even after cutting back so much, I've got hardly anything left."

"It's already subsidised, Mum. You don't exactly have to be rich to be able to afford it. The actual cost for the residential is £40 and the school is only asking us to pay £15."

"I know, love, but that's £15 I don't have."

I didn't believe it, so I did the number crunching myself. I subtracted the cost of bills and food from what Dad's pension paid out to Mum every month and she was right. Even on a tight budget, at the end of every week she was left with £7 or £8 after all of the necessary expenses.

The Geography field trip wasn't that important. I wasn't the only one who missed the trips because I couldn't afford to go. Nicolas (who lived on one of the canal boats) and Andrew (who never shared his answers in Science lessons) were two other students I knew who regularly missed trips because of money.

Most people at school were friendly and never said anything to us—except Razor and his pack of hooligans. Razor was also in Year 11 and had a rooster-style Mohican haircut, chest pushed forward, chains adorning his chest and wrists, slits in his right eyebrow and a diamond stud in his right ear. He went around the school intimidating everyone. Together with his four little minions, who tried so hard to impress him, they acted like they owned the school. Razor and two of his friends were unfortunately in my Geography class. He looked at us and shouted "tramps, tramps, tramps" every time the class left for the trips, leaving me, Nicolas and Andrew behind. We were sent to the Year 10 Geography class to quietly get on with 'independent work' whilst the rest of our class spent the whole day out on a field trip.

Every week we cut back on something in order to put money aside for the bills. Mum stopped buying branded items, always going for the cheaper supermarket and value ranges. She also stopped buying different types of things—now we only had one type of bread for our toast instead of croissants, cereal and porridge. Very soon, the rest of our meals followed and on two days a week we had soup for dinner. We never had any type of fruits in our house and sweets were non-existent. Drinks didn't exist in our house either: no fizz or juices. The only beverage we had was the water from our taps and even that we had to use in moderation because of the rising water rates. We tightened our belts until we felt the stranglehold on our bellies.

On most days, we stayed in one room so we didn't have to put the light on in the other rooms. On the colder days, we didn't turn on the central heating and went to bed with hot water bottles to keep us warm. Mum wrapped everyone up, including herself, in extra layers of clothes so we didn't feel the draught that had a way of creeping into the flat even though the doors and windows were closed.

We didn't have a television set. The widescreen Sony one Dad brought broke down and we couldn't afford to have it fixed. It was quite old so we didn't have a guarantee on it either. We didn't even throw it out. That old television just lay there like a dead corpse on the TV stand.

"Good thing, too," said Mum. "We can't afford the TV licence anyway, unless some money accidentally drops on our laps. I don't see that happening anytime soon."

"Mum, is there no way we can get that thing fixed?"

She sighed. "Nadim. I'm sure I don't need to explain to you again. You've done the maths and you know how we're managing. One thing, just one unexpected cost, could completely throw us off." She stared at the TV in disappointment and rubbed her forehead.

"Yeah I know, Mum, but haven't you got any emergency money? Did Dad not leave you anything?"

"He didn't leave much, darling. I used up that tiny bit of extra money we had over the last two Eids. I've got nothing left for the coming Eid this year."

After the TV broke down, we read books—loads of them. I borrowed whatever I could from my school and the local library for myself and Mum, and the twins had a good collection of children's books from their school. Mum and I read almost everything. Charles Dickens, Mary Shelley, Shakespeare, J.B. Priestley, Morris Glitzman, David Almond, Bram Stoker, books on Islamic history, stories of the Prophets—absolutely anything I could get my hands on for us. Mum sometimes read to all of us like our teacher did in primary school at 'reading time'. We all snuggled up next to her and she would read Roald Dahl's *Charlie and the Chocolate Factory* while we all listened, enthralled.

Reading was our escape from reality. Through reading, we found ourselves constantly in the company of kings, conquerors, ghosts, police inspectors, the rich, the poor and many men and women of knowledge and wisdom. I discovered that nothing else was able to fill my heart with so much joy and save me from boredom. We all took turns reading and always read in character. It was great to escape from our own minds and become somebody else. I quickly learnt new words and tried to use them in my

English lessons. I thought it made me sound intelligent but Mr Read, our English teacher, always raised an eyebrow when I (probably incorrectly) used a complex word.

School uniform had to last us more than a year. Mum told us to buy slightly bigger sizes so we could slowly grow into our shirts, trousers, jumpers and shoes. We had to also take special care of them and Mum would wash them once a week by hand in order to maintain their quality. We gave up on using the washing machine because it cost too much to run and maintain.

Towards the middle of the year we were forced to wear worn out clothes that didn't fit us properly. I didn't have a scientific calculator for my Maths lessons and so I filled out a form so the school could lend me one that the previous Year 11s donated to the school when they left. The school also gave me studded football shoes because Mum could only afford to buy me one pair of sports trainers, which were unsuitable for playing football on a grass pitch. Razor was always there in PE lessons sniggering at me as I struggled to play football with a slightly bigger pair of football boots. His head looked like a pineapple with shaved sides and spiked up hair.

"Don't worry, Niddy," he said, looking at me with his beady eyes and pointing at his shiny new football boots, "you can have this pair when I'm done. I'm getting those new Adidas Predators soon. I'll make these ones nice and smelly for you."

We weren't eligible for free school meals because of the pension so Mum paid Nusaybah and Nabeela's primary school directly at the beginning of every week and left me some money on the kitchen table every morning before I went to school. The lunch money paid to the twins' primary school meant that they had at least one full warm meal every day during the week, but the money Mum left for me wasn't enough even for the break time snacks let alone a full lunch from my school canteen. Their prices were extortionate, and they increased them again this year. I had just about enough to pay for a small slice of pizza and a small cookie. I usually had the cookie during break times and the slice of pizza at lunch time. They gave out free tap water in plastic cups so I didn't need to worry about buying a drink, but the food wasn't enough and I always felt hungry. I topped up with snacks that Graham and Ridwan sometimes gave out during the day from food that was left over from their packed lunches. I never told Mum—she was under so much stress already.

We didn't go to food banks and we didn't shop at charity shops, even though that would have eased the pressure on Mum a little.

"I can't do that!" she said.

Mum wasn't arrogant, but I guess she preferred to struggle a little than lose more of her dignity—she had already lost enough with Nabil in prison. People didn't understand. You don't get a choice in life regarding where you are born, what colour or religion you're born into and you certainly don't get a choice in who your family members are. But no one understood that you can't control who your family members are and the choices they make. Nabil should have understood, but he didn't. Now when people looked at us, they saw what he did. That's why Mum didn't go out much. I guess running a 'tight ship' at home and not reaching for the food banks and charity shops was Mum's way of still feeling some of the self-worth and dignity that she felt when Dad was around, which she lost much of due to the unforgiving and nosy people that lived around us. People whispered behind our backs, sniggered, gave us nasty looks and avoided bumping into any of us outside.

So, no. No food banks and no charity shops, even though things were really bad. I tried to convince Mum, but she wouldn't listen.

"Mum, we're eligible to go and I'm sure it will help. At least we can get most of the week's shopping done and free up your money for other things."

"No," she objected. "They don't make much difference, darling. They give you a can of beans, a tin of tuna and some veg and look at you like you're dirt from the bottom of their shoes."

"Mum, I'm sure it's not like that. A lot of students from my school go there to pick up stuff. They don't give you everything, but it definitely helps."

"No, we're not going. We're not that desperate yet. I bet they don't even have decent stuff there, just peoples' leftovers and donations," she said decidedly.

But that's not what I heard. Barry from my PE class said they give you crisps, fruits, chocolate and if you get there early enough on a Friday, they also give you pizza and garlic bread. His Dad went there every week. His family was struggling too, like so many other families in our area. Barry's dad was in a car accident last year and hurt his back really badly. He was on so many different painkillers and couldn't work to provide for his family. They lost their home and had to move into a smaller place. They were still on the council waiting list to be housed, but it shouldn't take long, Barry told me, because his Dad has some priority because of his disability.

I decided to check out our local food bank. Not to get anything from there because Mum forbade me from doing so, but just to see how they were helping people. I was amazed at the mechanical way it functioned. It was so busy—the volunteers were running around packing things into bags and placing them into small boxes, ready to hand them over to people depending on what they needed. The queues were longer than theme park ride queues and often stretched around the entire Stoke Community Centre building. The people waiting in those queues all looked very dishevelled. They held the social services recommendation letters in their hands (without it the food bank wouldn't give you anything), and constantly looked at their watches, probably because they were exhausted by the long wait. There were mostly families with small children in the queues. They all had this eerie, blank look on their faces as their eyes fixated on the back of the person ahead of them. They just stared mindlessly, waiting for the queue to shorten.

I saw a couple with their three children waiting in the line. The father wore a dirty, grey tracksuit with holes in the knee area and the mother wore a simple lime green dress with trainers and no socks. The children had clearly outgrown their clothes and constantly chewed their sleeves. They seemed agitated by the long wait and couldn't keep still. The youngest child kept sliding off her pushchair and running off, only for the father to run after her, place her back into the buggy, strap her in and re-join the queue. He kept biting his lips, scratching his face and reaching for his wife's wrist to look at her watch.

"Not long now, we're almost there," he repeated like a programmed robot. Since I wasn't queuing for food, I left them to walk into the building, sliding past the volunteers who were struggling to control the crowd and keep everyone in an orderly queue.

Once I got into the building, I noticed that the volunteers all looked cheery and enthusiastic as they rushed around, trying to get as many people through their doors in the quickest possible time. Inside there was tinned food, cereal, bread, fruit, vegetables, dried fruit, frozen foods and a huge line of different packets of porridge. There were also two small vans parked outside, which brought in donated food from the local supermarkets. One section was also cordoned off and made into a soup kitchen, which operated on Monday and Thursday mornings. A strange combination of different smells hung in the air along with a prominent smell of tomato soup. The soups were all made in their kitchen with the leftover vegetables from the food bank so there were no empty cans to clear out, just lots of large plastic cups they used to serve the soup and small paper plates used for the bread and crusty rolls.

There was another room at the back with WORK SKILLS written in huge letters across the top. They held workshops to help people get back into work and back on their feet again. They helped with things like CV writing, interview skills, how to search for jobs, how to write out good application forms and how to approach potential employers in different sectors through networking. Outside the room was a huge notice board with a few adverts for different jobs, skills training sessions, support sessions and even drugs counselling sessions. These guys were doing an amazing job, I thought.

I bumped into Musa whilst I was there. With his sleeves rolled up, he got stuck in, preparing food packs for people. I noticed a long scar on his right forearm and a partially concealed tattoo further up. I'm sure there was an interesting story behind both, I thought to myself, but I couldn't ask him about it. Sweat trickled down his forehead as he took the next order, running from one place to another in order to prepare another box for a different family. His eyes caught sight of me.

"*Asalamu-alaykum*, Nadim. How you doing, bro?" he asked, wiping the sweat off his forehead. "Is someone preparing a pack for you?"

"*Wa-alaykum salam*," I replied. "Nah, I didn't come to get anything. I was just passing by and thought I'd pop in. You guys are doing a great job *mashallah*." I was mesmerised. I couldn't help but stare at the shelves and containers that were quickly emptying out.

"Gotta do what we can, man. A lot of families are going hungry, you know... you'd be surprised at how much poverty there is around here. Just glad I can do my bit. It's important for us as Muslims to do what we can." He scanned his eyes around, searching for the next item. "You look a bit troubled, man, what's up?" he asked.

"Nothing," I replied plainly.

"Nah, come on, don't give me that!" he urged with a warm smile. "I tell you what... just hang around for a bit, I'm almost done. We can go to the mosque and pray *maghrib* together inshallah. Come back in about an hour and I'll be done, okay?"

"I can't today, sorry. I've got a bit of homework I need to finish off."

"Alright, next time then inshallah."

"Deffo, inshallah." I left him to it.

Mum had no choice, however, but to visit Mell Street Market, a second-hand market that opened every Saturday, right behind my secondary school. It contained stalls where people sold almost anything: clothes, old coins, toys, DVDs and absolutely anything they wanted to get rid of. It was like a huge car boot sale. A lot of people we knew went there, but one of the unwritten rules was that people didn't speak to one another if they happened to bump into each other at Mell Street, even if they knew each other. I guess it was the shame and embarrassment of people knowing they had to shop in a second-hand market. Maybe this way, they could keep on denying that they were truly struggling.

I often saw a girl from my old primary school there. Her name was Riya, a very sporty, thin girl of average height who used to sit right opposite me when we were in class together. She reminded me a bit of Sigourney Weaver from the Alien films and I used to imagine her armed to the teeth shooting different zombies and aliens. Her dad was also there early on Saturday morning searching through the clothes stalls and picking up items for Riya and her family. Riya looked at me, but never made eye contact if I looked back at her. She always had a dreamy, distant look in her eyes. We often bumped into each other on our way to and from secondary school as our paths crossed. Sometimes she would be with her friends, but on the occasions she walked alone, she stopped to say hello and make polite conversation. We talked about our school work and other stuff, but we never spoke about seeing each other at Mell Street Market. She never mentioned it and neither did I.

When mum was really short, she also took items from the Community Fridge at our local corner shop. The shopkeeper, Mr Cooper, put a second fridge freezer next to the normal fridge where he kept the stock that he sold. That second fridge was called the 'Community Fridge' where people placed items inside it that they wished to donate, the way they did for food banks. Everyone knew about the Community Fridge. It was brimming with donations of milk, soft drinks, yoghurt, cream cakes, lemon tarts and a whole range of other goodies. All the items were clearly labelled so Mr Cooper knew not to charge you for them when you brought them to the till. There was a limit on how much you could take from the fridge each week: two items per week for individuals and five items for families.

The Community Fridge made a huge difference to our lives and the lives of many families who were struggling in our community. Such was the impact of Mr Cooper's genius idea that other shopkeepers around the country soon followed him, and it featured on the local news too.

Mr Cooper was very proud of himself and posed in front of the cameras every time one of the newspaper photographers came to his shop. I always thought he was a very shy man—he seemed that way at first. He was always very quiet and rarely made any conversation when anyone went to his shop. But that soon changed with his new-found 'fame'.

"I'm just doing my bit for the community. We're all in this together. Gotta help each other out," he said, posing with his thumbs up and a huge smile almost as wide as the fridge behind him. But behind this short-lived 'fame' was another struggling individual trying to keep afloat. With the sudden increase in business rates, small shops on our road began to close one by one. People were talking about one of the big retailers bribing the local councillors to hike up the business rates so they wouldn't be able to pay the rent, making it easier for the big retailers to buy them out. Mr Cooper hung in there for dear life even when things got really bad. Luckily for him someone started a crowd-funding campaign to support him. His fame helped and the donations kept pouring in—that made it on the news too. By the end of the week, he had enough money to pay the shop's rent for the next six months. So he was safe for a while. He used the remaining donations to give out free bottled water every time there was a water leak in the neighbourhood, which happened almost every two months because the water companies didn't maintain the pipes properly.

My time at the food bank and Mr Cooper's shop was an illuminating experience. It was incredible to see where all the donated food was going and seeing people working hard together to help those in need. I felt a real sense of community, of normal people doing what they could despite their own difficulties to help those less fortunate. When I saw people in more difficult positions than us, I was thankful that despite our own difficulties, we were still able to keep our head above water and weren't completely sinking, despite running a tight ship. It strengthened my determination and resolve to keep upbeat and positive. I wasn't prepared to give up—not yet, anyway.

Chapter 7

The Red Letter Day

I found Mum in tears in the morning. This time she didn't bother to wipe them away—they gushed freely down her face. She was holding a letter in her right hand. One of those red letters I remember only too well. Some things never seem to go away. Some experiences stay with you forever and seem to repeat themselves, over and over.

"I can't take any more," she sobbed. "I don't know how much longer I can do this for." She placed her right hand on her chest and tried to slow down her breathing. I brought her some water and told her to sip slowly. This was what happened when Mum worried or stressed out too much. She found it difficult to breathe, her chest tightened up and I would need to bring her inhaler immediately otherwise she could have a panic attack.

She was so patient with everything and placed her trust in Allah, but Mum also had a way of bottling things up inside which wasn't good for her. I tried to calm her down, but I sensed that she wanted to be left alone. She got used to that after Dad passed away. So I left her to go to school, hoping she would be feeling better when I came back.

I walked to school, listening to the birds chirping in the trees above me and the dried-up, brown autumn leaves crunching beneath my feet. I often decided not to take the bus when I wanted to clear my head. Walking past a row of sheds, I saw a few boarded up flats in a medium-rise tower block. It must be another one of those buildings the council were planning to break down and turn into luxury flats, I thought, before turning around to be met with a pair of prominent, light brown eyes. It was Riya. She greeted me with her usual smile. She always looked very simple. There were no traces of make-up on her face apart from pink lip gloss, unlike most of the girls at my school who came in heavily made up like they were going to a wedding. It was like they were trying to hide something, mask something away beneath several layers of removable coating. But not Riya.

"Hey there," she called in her usual soft voice.

"Hi." I smiled back. "Riya?"

"Yeah, come on, you haven't forgotten my name have you?" she laughed, flicking her eyes upwards again. "How are you?"

"Yeah, I'm good. And you?"

"Yeah, I'm alright. Not enjoying this cold to be honest. It just seems to get colder every winter."

"Yeah I know, got to wrap up and stay warm I guess." It was always nice to see Riya. She reminded me of my primary school years, and those years were some of the happiest moments of my life. Dad was still around, Mum was a lot happier and Nabil was still with us.

My mind started drifting off, thinking about Mum.

"You okay, Nadim?" she asked. I looked at her smooth skin, clear as the raindrops that fell on her dark eyelashes and full, heart-shaped lips. Her hazel eyes gave me a strange look. "You don't seem yourself?" she added, her forehead creasing with concern.

"I'm fine. I've just got a lot on, you know, with school and stuff."

"Yeah, tell me about it! Anyway, I need to go," she said, waving at her two giggling friends across the road, who were calling her over. "Take care, see you." For some strange reason I felt empty as I watched Riya walk towards her friends and disappear into the distance. I didn't know why I felt sad, but I did, as if I was waiting for something terrible to happen.

* * *

The daylight was slowly fading away as I walked back from school. I heard the rustling of a squirrel as it climbed the trees searching for food, making the autumn leaves drop gently on the ground. In the distance, I caught sight of Musa walking towards me.

"Asalamu-alaykum bro. Just on my way to the mosque to pray maghrib. Why don't you join me?" he asked, his smile warming up the cold autumn evening. I didn't really want to go. I had a lot playing on my mind since leaving Mum in the morning and I just wanted to get home. But how could I resist his cheery face and welcoming smile?

"Maghrib is in five minutes," he added before I could answer, "I'm sure homework can wait a little." He wasn't assertive or forceful, just friendly and encouraging. I had no choice but to give in.

"Yeah sure, let's go."

The melodious sound of the *adhaan* was already reverberating around the walls of the mosque when we entered. I quickly made my way through the dark corridor and into the ablution room to make wudu. As the cold water washed over my hands, nose, mouth, arms, face, head and feet, I felt a sense of calm return to my body.

The Imam started the prayer and I quickly joined the row behind Musa, which quickly began to fill up with other latecomers. I said my *takbir* and tried to focus on the *salaah*. The outside world ceased to exist as I absorbed the smooth and pleasing voice of the Imam. After a while I stopped trying to break down some of the Arabic words that I knew and began to lose myself in the moment, only to be suddenly awoken as the Imam went into prostration. After the prayer, I saw Musa getting up to offer the *sunnah* prayers. I wanted to use that opportunity to make du'a to Allah. Raising my hands close to my chest, I cupped my hands and pushed them out, as if I was a beggar asking for them to be filled. I didn't plan a particular du'a. I just said whatever came to my mind.

"Oh Allah," I pleaded. "Please give me strength. Help my mum. Help our family. Support us in this time of distress. Surely there is no one to help us except You." I continued like this for what seemed like a very long time. I felt a raging storm slowly develop within my chest. I felt the tears, but I grit my teeth and suppressed them—I didn't want Musa to see me like that.

After the prayers we slowly walked home. The night was clear, the wind had slowed and the air was silent. I was so lost in my own thoughts that I almost forgot that Musa was walking next to me through the leafy pathway that led back to our estate.

"Nadim, what's up, bro?" he asked. "And don't say it's nothing. I saw you after we finished salaah."

I wasn't good at hiding things or bottling them up inside like Mum did. My face was an open book that anybody could read. "Things aren't that great at home," I told him. "It's been so difficult since my dad passed away. Nabil is behind bars, money is really tight, my mum's always stressed, I'm falling behind at school and... and... I don't really know what to do." I tried not to let him see me get emotional. "I want to help and support my mum and the twins as much as possible, but I don't know how to. I just wish Nabil was here."

"I'm really sorry to hear that, bro, but try to stay strong and stay positive. Your mum and those little girls need you."

"I'm trying, believe me I am, but sometimes I wake up feeling like my family is going to collapse and fall apart, like we're on a speeding train waiting to crash."

"Don't say stuff like that, bro. I know we ain't really spoken about Nabil. I wanted to, but I didn't in case you felt uncomfortable. From what I know of him, he'll be alright—he can handle himself."

"He can't cope in prison, trust me. Underneath that 'hard man' attitude, he's a real softie."

"He'll be fine. He'll learn to adapt, he'll cope. You just focus on your family. As for your studies, you make sure you stay on top of the game, alright? You don't wanna leave school with nothing and get sucked in by those street rats." I felt a sense of anger rising his voice. "Trust me, I've been there. Fortunately, allhamdulillah, I was able to get out of it, but not everyone is that lucky. They make you do things like nicking things from shops, robbing people on the streets and snatching handbags from old women to go up in their 'ranks'—and that's just the beginning! I'm not proud of the things I've done. If that wasn't bad enough the older guys use you to move drugs around different neighbourhoods and collect money from addicts, the 'repeat customers'. *Wallahi* bro, I regret every bad thing I did, every second of my time that I spent with them. They use you, abuse you and then chuck you to the side when they don't need you anymore!"

"How did you manage to get away from them?" I asked.

"Prison, bro, prison," he replied, shaking his head. "They started upping their game by doing burglaries to make more money. In the end it was me who got pulled in and busted when the police raided my flat, not them. Time in prison made me think, reflect and contemplate. I met many brothers who were once like me, but now wanted to change their lives, change their priorities and do the right thing. That's when I rediscovered the jewel that I was already given even though I didn't deserve it: Islam."

"That's deep." I admired his courage to speak about his experiences. "They do all that for money but it doesn't mean anything in the end. Although I do wish I was born rich like some people," I muttered under my breath. "That would be really handy."

"I'm sure we all wish that, but the world doesn't work like that," he laughed, stroking his beard. "You just have to adapt, make adjustments and try and live within your means. Everyone is facing those difficulties. If you want, I can get you in touch with someone who can help your mum budget more efficiently. Sometimes it's just a case of making small adjustments here and there that could make a lot of difference to you. There's a lot of support down the Stoke Community Centre if you want me to step in."

"Nah, we're okay for now," I said, "but thanks." I didn't have the energy to explain how many 'adjustments' we had already made.

"Allah tests everyone, bro—the good and the bad. That's just how this life is. You have to try and stay strong, make du'a and do what you can to help yourself. That's when the help of Allah will come."

I knew he was right. He made a lot of sense, but it was just hard implementing it. We both said our goodbyes before entering our separate flats, in the tower block we called home.

* * *

I found Mum searching through her bedroom cupboards in a frenzy. "I still have the gold your dad gave me when we got married." She sniffed, letting her tears flow down her cheeks. "It's not a lot—not enough to make us rich," she said, trying to force a smile, "but if I manage to sell it, we will probably get a couple of thousand."

Another miracle, I thought to myself. Alhamdulillah, we've been saved again! The money would certainly help!

That night, I felt an immense sense of relief. I looked outside from my bedroom window. The moonlight covered the calm stillness of the water and the autumn leaves slowly collected themselves along the sides like tinned sardines. I saw a couple walking along the footpath wearing their winter coats with their scarves wrapped around their necks and their gloved hands interlocking each other's to provide another layer of warmth on the breezy night. They looked comfortable. For the first time in a long time, I felt comfortable too.

Having fallen asleep suddenly, I was woken up by the sound of Mum's faint voice. It was around 2am. Way too early for anyone to be up for *fajr*. I could hear muffled sounds and deep voices along with heavy footsteps pacing around the living room and kitchen.

I put on my robe and slowly tread across the corridor.

"We understand how distressing this is for you, ma'am, and I'm very sorry you have had to go through this," said a firm and mechanical voice. "We understand that you're shaken, but the window has been sealed and for now there's nothing else we can do. Over the last few years our budgets have been halved and chopped at every department, including our burglary department. I'm afraid that we don't have the resources to follow up these incidents. Please sleep in one of your children's rooms tonight, ma'am," he continued.

As I reached the living room, I saw two very tall police officers standing there with their notepads out, looking very serious. Their pointy hats were sat on the coffee table like two small black cats.

We were burgled along with three other flats on our block that night. The burglars broke into Mum's bedroom and managed to get in through her window, which she often left slightly open for air to get in to prevent any potential panic attacks during the night.

The alarm didn't go off because Mum stopped paying the subscription months ago so they disabled it. The burglars only left after Mum abruptly woke up. She didn't scream. She just froze and watched quietly as they helped themselves to the money from her purse and the gold jewellery she left out from the evening.

We were back to square one! That was the final stroke for Mum. She let out a wail and slumped down on the sofa, unable to move or speak.

What could I do? How was I going to cope without her?

I looked upwards to the sky wanting to make du'a to Allah. I raised my hands, but I couldn't bring myself to say anything. The shock of the whole situation stiffened my body and left me speechless. I looked around the room, staring at everyone's faces, wanting them to say something that brought some ease to my heart. The room was silent.

"Officer," I said desperately, "she's going to be okay, right?"

"We've called an ambulance," he replied in a grim and formal tone. "I'm sure she'll be fine. The ambulance is coming to check her over."

"Please, you have to do something. You can't just leave her like that."

"She'll be fine, young man," said the other police officer. "It's just the shock. It must have been a bit too much for her. The ambulance is on its way, we've already radioed for it."

Musa and his mum heard the commotion and ran straight into the living room. "What's happened here?" she asked, placing her hand on Mum's head. "Is she okay?" She looked at the police officers, trying to make sense of the situation.

I waited for the ambulance to arrive and sat next to Mum as she lay on the sofa, completely unconscious. Her body was limp. She was completely lifeless. By this time,

Nabeela and Nusaybah had also woken up and ran into the living room looking petrified. I felt an urge to put my arms around them, comfort them, tell them everything was going to be okay... but I didn't know if it would be.

Chapter 8

The Man of the House

It was a misty morning. A crow perched on a tree just outside the St Christopher's Hospital, its loud caws piercing the cold air. As soon as we pulled up to the entrance of the Accident & Emergency department, I ran in, leaving everyone else behind. My heart was pounding. I had no idea what state she would be in. I ran from one cubicle to another—she was nowhere to be seen. I went to the main desk where the doctors were all located and searched for her name on the notice board. My eyes frantically scanned up and down and left to right.

"I need to find my mum!" I burst out, looking around like a lost child in a shopping centre.

"Name, please," replied a nurse in dark blue uniform. Before I could answer, I caught a glimpse of Mum's dark beige *hijab* through the glass window in the room just in front of the reception desk. I didn't waste any time. I ran, straight to her side. I didn't wake her. I just sat there, watching her. She looked almost peaceful. Musa, his mum and the twins soon joined us.

"I've gotta get to work, bro, my shift's starting soon," said Musa, placing his right hand on my shoulder. "Mum's staying with you lot, but if you need me for anything, just drop me a text or call, yeah?"

"Thanks. Thank you for driving us in."

"It's no trouble at all, bro. You stay strong and make du'a. Aunty will be just fine, inshallah."

We didn't go to school. The four of us sat surrounding Mum's bed as she lay there helplessly, still unconscious. We were hungry—we hadn't had any breakfast that morning so we shared the hospital food they gave to Mum between us. I'll get some for Mum when she wakes up, I told myself. Musa's mum also bought us some drinks and sandwiches from the local Tesco Express.

I spent most of the morning silently praying, crying and pleading to Allah to cure Mum and bring her back to us.

She finally did come around late that afternoon.

"What's happening?" she gasped. "Where am I? What's going on? What is all of this?" She pointed to the various leads that went into the catheter on her right arm.

"Your sugar levels were really low, Mum," I explained. "They had to pump you with this stuff to wake you up."

"Oh, Nadim. I'm sorry." She suddenly burst into tears. Musa's mum took her hand.

"You've got nothing to be sorry about, Mum," I reassured her.

"I'm sorry for scaring you all like that. I need to be stronger, for all of you."

"Mum, it isn't your fault! You didn't scare us—well, maybe just a bit—but you're okay now and we can get you home."

She lay back down and calmed herself. She looked at our faces. I didn't recognise the look in her eyes. For the first time, she looked defeated. She went on to explain what happened the previous night.

"I didn't see them creep in," she explained, shaking her head. "It was my fault. I shouldn't have left the window open. When I opened my eyes, I saw them rummaging through everything. There were two of them. They were wearing balaclavas and those big biker helmets. I couldn't say anything. I just froze and let them get on with it. It was only when they saw the gold that I left out earlier that I begged 'No, please, no!' and the taller one looked at me with his big, scary eyes and threatened to harm us." She started crying. "So I promised not to scream as long as they left us alone. It was long after they left that I forced myself up and called the police. As I finished speaking to them, I felt my heart racing. I dropped the phone because I couldn't breathe properly. By the time the police arrived, I was really struggling. When I looked up at them, what just happened finally dawned on me—that's when I went into complete panic mode. I lost control. The last thing I remember is one of the police officers handing me some water and telling me to remain calm. Everything went blank after that."

"It's okay, Mum. Everything is going to be okay." I swallowed hard, hoping I'd convinced her.

* * *

"Mummy, I want to go home," pleaded Nabeela. The twins became restless by the late afternoon.

"We will go home, guys," I told them both. "We just need Mum to get better."

"What's wrong with Mum?" asked Nusaybah.

"She's fine, darling." Musa's mum stroked Nusaybah's hair. "She's just had a little scare, that's all. You know how sometimes you have a bad dream and get a little scared? Everything is going to be fine. We'll get your mummy home inshallah, just as soon as the doctors check her over."

It wasn't Mum's fault. Burglaries were on the increase—loads of blocks on our street had been burgled over the last few months. It mostly happened to the flats on the ground floor, until people started putting iron bars on their doors and windows. That's when the burglars changed their tactics. You never really think it will happen to you until it does.

The red letter Mum had received the previous morning was from the gas company. They accidentally undercharged us on our gas bill as there had been a mix-up with another address.

The bill was for around nine hundred pounds.

Her stress levels were already very high. The burglary and that horrid demand letter must have been all too much for her. You can never truly understand what other people are going through. I could only imagine. The strain of raising three children on very little money, the loneliness after losing Dad, and the shame of Nabil being in prison must have weighed heavy on her heart. I won't ever really know what that felt like. She kept it together, but occasionally it got too much for her.

Mum's pale face concealed her emerging wrinkles, but did nothing to cover her drooping dark under eye bags, which made her look like she hadn't slept in her entire life. I watched Mum's face as she lay there on the hospital bed. She looked down and took her inhaler every few minutes. She looked lifeless, as if someone had sucked all of the energy out of her body. She ran her fingers through her hair, which was once upon a time thick and full of volume, but now was slowly thinning and peppered with grey strands.

"I didn't realise it was going to be this difficult," she whimpered, wiping her tears and trying her best not to cry. "Your dad left me at such a young age. I need him. I need him so much."

"We all need him, Mum," I said, my voice beginning to break. I tried to hold back my tears, but it was no use—they fell from my eyes, hot and heavy on my cheeks. I tried to keep it together, to appear strong in front of Mum, but at that point I couldn't do it. The tears fell freely, gathering at the bottom of my neck like a dripping water leak. It felt almost like a relief, like they were washing out the pain.

"I know it was Allah's Decree, but sometimes," Mum continued, "sometimes I just find it so difficult. Then I look at all of you, my babies, and then the struggle seems to be worth it." She began to cry uncontrollably again.

"We're all here for you, Mum. I'm here for you and I'm not leaving anytime soon inshallah," I reassured her, still trembling.

"I know, baby, and I don't know what I would do without you." She looked up at me. "You're so much like your dad. So strong and caring mashallah."

I wiped away my tears, put my arms around the twins and took Mum's hand. I kissed her forehead and held her close to my chest.

"We're all in this together, Mum, and inshallah Allah will help us."

"I know," she replied, wiping her eyes and nose. She didn't say anything else. She just held us, containing all of us in her tiny arms.

* * *

I had to grow up even more after that night and I tried my best to look after Mum and the twins. It definitely wasn't easy being 'man of the house'.

Long after that night, I kept having flashbacks. It was terrifying. Mum started breathing very heavily. The two police officers tried to keep her calm, but their presence must have added to her anxiety. Her face went red. I saw her struggling. I tried to calm her myself. The police officers radioed for an ambulance, which came within minutes. They came up to our flat and tried to keep her conscious by talking to her and giving her oxygen to help her breathe, but nothing changed. She eventually passed out, bringing back all the memories of what happened when Dad was ill. My heart sank as I watched in horror as they lifted my mum onto a makeshift wheelchair and took her down the stairs and into the ambulance. I didn't know what to do or what to expect. I grit my teeth, clenched my fists, rubbed my face and tried to keep myself calm. I felt like a little incredible hulk was inside of me waiting to burst out! I wanted to cry, I wanted to shout out loud, and I wanted to smash everything around me, but I couldn't. I had to remain calm.

That red letter! It felt like a boxing glove, landing a huge blow. I hated it. I wanted to rip it up and burn it on the flames of our old cooker, even though I knew that wouldn't make any difference. It was the stupid gas company. It was their fault. But what do they care about families? We were just another figure on their computer screens who owed them money, and they would just send out threatening red letters until we paid up.

70

I tried to call the 0800 number they provided on top of the bill but even after waiting for over an hour, they were still passing me from one person to another. No one seemed to be able to help me!

Things were often like this: surrounded by a stupid system where you couldn't talk to the right person. The call handlers (who were probably based in another country) knew very little and only dealt with simple enquiries. They passed me on to their supervisors, who could only help with the smallest of complaints like an error in the meter reading, so they passed me on to their managers. After spending a further thirty minutes explaining myself to them, these managers told me write in to their 'complaints department', which didn't even have a contact number—only a PO Box address somewhere in Manchester. It was enough to make you want to give up.

"Whatever you need, bro, I'm there," Musa said when I bumped into him at the mosque later that week. "Anytime you need to run any errands for your mum, get the shopping done, pick up a prescription, whatever it is, you let me know, okay?"

"Thanks," I said absent-mindedly. I sighed. "Money. Just because of money, my mum's been in this state. She was scared and stressed because of a bill and then the robbery just sent her over the edge." I looked out of the mosque window, watching the rain fall dismally, slapping the pavement hard. It slammed on the moving vehicles outside as grey clouds and a thick fog began to develop. Shaking, I curled my fists up in anger. "Errand," I said slowly. "Maybe I could run some 'errands' for the street boys. At least I could make some money. I just need a few quid to help my mum out a little."

"Stop it," said Musa, his voice soft but firm. He put his arm on my shoulder. "Calm down. I know you're hurt and this must be really difficult for you, in ways that I can't imagine. But let me tell you one thing, bro, you guys have already lost your dad, and your brother for a short while. If you love your mum and sisters, stay away from those 'street rats', cos if you don't, you'll end up either in jail or dead before you even reach eighteen. Do you understand? Stay the hell away from that lot. I lost three years of my life cos of them, you know that. And now your brother is losing precious years of his life cos of them too." I didn't say anything to him. I just looked at his face. I knew he was right. I would do anything to make things easier, but I knew doing the wrong thing wasn't an option.

"Your family needs you. Never make the wrong choices. What would happen to your family if anything happened to you?" He didn't need to convince me much. I knew he was right. I just needed to find some strength from somewhere. "Allah will provide and make things easy. Trust me. Just be patient. The storm will pass eventually—it always does. Nothing is forever!"

I looked again out of the window. I saw the radiance of the street-lamps against the backdrop of the small pellets of raindrops, creating a glowing neon light. The rain suddenly ceased and the air was drying up, but the streets were still damp. The silence was so soothing, enough to drown out my anxiety. There was more rain to come before the skies fully cleared, but for now I just stood there, taking it all in.

Chapter 9

Street Boys

Mum wasn't her usual self after coming out of the hospital. She seemed more fragile than ever and she mostly stayed at home. I took the twins to school in the morning, even though it was in the opposite direction of my school. I did the weekly shopping and even cooked for everyone some evenings. I cooked mostly simple things like pasta bake, jacket potatoes and sandwiches. I had to take out money from the cash machine for Mum—that was always a nerve-racking experience. I walked through a quiet alleyway into our estate, passing the street boys before I got into our building and upstairs into our flat.

Passing by the street boys was the scariest part of the journey. We called them 'street boys' because that's exactly what they were. Most of them were school dropouts who were used by the older boys on the estate to carry 'stuff', usually drugs and stolen goods.

Dad always told us to stay away from them, so that's exactly what I did. I didn't know that Nabil was slowly and secretly warming to them when Dad became really unwell. The street boys even looked strange, like they were always on edge, always looking around as if someone was watching them. They dropped off and picked up stolen goods, sold drugs wrapped up in cling film, passed things from hand to hand with other street boys, who then passed things to older guys in expensive cars. We stayed well clear of them and got on with our lives and thank God they never approached us for anything. But it would have been very tempting if they asked you to join them. It came with a type of 'cred' and 'respect' that everyone on the estate recognised. Even in school, everyone knew people like Razor were linked to the street boys. Nobody messed with him, not even the teachers, out of fear of what their outside back up could do. For me it wasn't the respect or the credibility that was tempting, it was the money and how much they had of it. They threw it around like Monopoly money, buying whatever they wanted, when they wanted. The rest of us 'honest' people made adjustments and cut-backs just to survive. But not the street boys. They had the latest phones, luxury designer clothes and expensive trainers. Even their families knew what they were up to, but I doubt they said anything to them. Everyone was on survival mode and people were doing whatever they could to get through the storm, including turning a blind eye to what their children were getting up to on the streets.

* * *

As the days passed, Mum looked more and more unwell. She had a cocktail of pills and tablets next to her bedroom table, which had been damaged from the burglary. We couldn't replace it so we just put some cardboard under one of the legs to stop it from falling over.

When I forced Mum to come and sit with us, she looked like she was sinking into the sofa, as if it was slowly swallowing her up. She looked smaller and frailer than ever before, especially when she forgot to take her medication. When she did take all of her medication on time, she was happy and jolly, which sometimes scared me because she wasn't her usual self then either. She sometimes became ecstatic and talked way too much. I guess that was the medication. I just wanted my mum back. But with her current state, I didn't count on getting her back any time soon. I just tried to keep calm and carry on. What else could I do?

Patience and hoping for the best was the only tool I had to keep fighting, but deep down I felt the effects of everything. I couldn't stop my mind from thinking of the endless negative consequences that could come to be if anything happened to Mum, even though some of these thoughts were completely irrational and highly unlikely. It was as if my brain was an endless maze. The restlessness and lack of sleep made my body ache, and when I did fall asleep I woke up to the sound of the alarm clock, feeling sick. I'd look to my right to see Nabil's empty, neatly made-up single bed. It hadn't been slept on for such a long time.

I battled with my heart and mind every night. It was particularly bad when I was by myself, which is why I stayed up with Mum and the twins as late as possible.

"I have to stop this. I have to get a grip," I told myself. "I'm the man of the house!"

For a while I asked myself: Am I going mad? Am I going to start to have panic attacks like Mum? Do I need to see a doctor? The only thing I knew I did need was for all the problems to go away. I needed my old mum back. I needed our money problems to sort out. I needed that horrible red letter to disappear and I needed Nabil back.

I knew these problems wouldn't go away by themselves. I had to work hard on them and remain patient.

Sometimes I didn't want to fight anymore. I was sick and tired of life. Sick and tired of the storm of problems that came our way, but I couldn't give up. What alternative did I have? Take my own life (that thought did come to my mind very briefly, but I quickly dismissed it). That wasn't the answer. Life is a gift from Allah the Almighty, and much too precious to throw away. What would happen to my family if I wasn't around? I couldn't even imagine.

I forced myself to stop. I made istighfaar and found some peace through it, managing to calm my troubled heart by *dhikr*.

I fell asleep, only to be abruptly awoken by a loud noise coming from outside. I was a light sleeper as it was— any small bit of sound woke me up. I woke up gasping for air, my hand on my chest, trying to ease my breathing. My pillow was soaked with sweat and a sticky, wet feeling prickled my body. I sat up on my bed for a few minutes, panting and wondering where that sound was coming from. Finally, I felt my heart slow down to a regular rhythm again and the air reached my lungs.

I got up to look outside. My netted curtains were drawn, so I pulled up the blinds. I felt the small gusts of wind coming through the poorly insulated edges of my bedroom window. I could see them clearly now. They operated quietly and seamlessly, but there was always the odd occasional shout from one of them every time they saw a patrolling police car coming into the estate. In the distance, I saw a big white car waiting by the construction site where a new set of luxury flats were being built.

The lights were turned off, but I saw someone waiting inside the car like a tiger in stealth mode. There was a group of street boys walking towards the car, but others were walking away like they were being pulled by a strange wave that contained currents in the opposite direction. There was obviously something going on, but I didn't know what, nor did I want to. I had more important things to think about.

I decided to make wudu with cold water, which had a strangely refreshing feeling and prayed two *rakats* of prayer. It was late at night and well before the fajr prayers. I made du'a at every opportunity: in *ruku*, in *sujood*, and as I sat towards the end of the prayer. I then raised my hands to the heavens in yearning and expectation.

"Ya Allah," I cried. "I know everything is from You. I know I am Your creation and I have no right to question what You do to me, but I ask You, my Lord, please bring us some ease. Bring some ease from places I haven't even imagined due to the limited mind You have blessed me with. You are strong, oh Allah, whilst I am weak; You are able, oh Allah, whilst I am incapable of doing anything. You are the responder to all du'as whilst I am the caller. Please answer my du'as and have mercy on me and my family. Bring about ease and comfort to our hardship and suffering *ya* Allah. I beg You! I am desperate for Your love and mercy! There is no God but You!"

By pouring my heart out to Allah, I felt a lot better. I had a sense that in the end, everything was going to be okay. I just needed to let go and fully trust in Him. I needed to find a sense of calm in the chaos and wait, because I knew that Allah is with those who are patient.

Chapter 10

My Escape

I was in a routine: drop off the twins to school in the morning, go to school myself, pick up the shopping on the way back, collect the twins from homework club, prepare some food for dinner and make sure Mum had taken her medication.

I tried to make school my escape. I was falling behind, but I'd always done well at school. I enjoyed pretty much all of my subjects, especially English. School was the one thing that kept me occupied so my mind didn't wander off and dwell on any of my other problems.

I had a good set of friends. There was Graham, a blond-haired, pale boy who arrived here from Germany a few years ago after his dad was transferred to London by the tech company he worked for. Graham was as sharp as a knife, especially in Maths, which was my weakest subject. There was Hisham, who arrived the previous year from Barcelona. His English wasn't great, but he was amazing in languages, mainly because he was already fluent in five different ones: Arabic, French, Spanish, Italian and Berber (which he told us was an ancient language spoken by some people in Morocco). Nayeem was brilliant in Physics and wanted to become a pilot, Ridwan wanted to become a businessman and always thought in numbers and figures, Zahir who was into photo and video editing and then there was Bilal, who just wanted to finish school as quickly as possible so he could do an apprenticeship with a big company. A steady job and good money was all he was after.

We all got along and had nicknames for each other: Graham was the 'General' because he always walked with his back straight and his mum made sure that his school uniform and shiny shoes looked flawless; Nayeem was 'Captain' because he wanted to be a pilot and often went as close as he could to the City Airport to do some 'plane spotting'; Hisham was 'Hash' because he ate hash browns with everything—his breakfast, his burgers and he even snacked on them throughout the day; Ridwan was 'Redz' because of the way his face turned dark red when he was nervous about something, which happened often; Zahir was 'Zero' because he was incredibly thin and never put on any weight whatever he ate and we were all secretly very jealous of him; Bilal was 'Bells' because he kept on losing his keys and so his mum forced him to clip it to his belt using a huge keyring, which made a ringing sound wherever he walked. And me, well they called me Crix, because I was the only one out of us to be able to 'crack' the Rubik's cube by completing it in the quickest time. I learnt it from a video clip I saw some time ago and practised it until I perfected it. We were all very different and must have seemed like an odd bunch, but we had more things in common that bound us together.

You need a good set of friends to get you through school, which sometimes functioned like the mafia. You had a hierarchy with the Headteacher and the deputies and assistants right at the top—they were the 'big dons'. Then came the teachers and support staff, with us students right at the bottom of the pecking order. School was all about survival of the fittest. If you studied hard, stayed out of trouble and kept your head down you could leave school with a pretty decent education and then go on to college and university if you wanted. But if you left with nothing, then you couldn't choose what you wanted to do next. You could either get a dead-end job and continue with that until you were 70 or turn into a street boy until the police caught up with you.

The best part of school was chilling with your mates and teasing them about how badly you beat them on Fifa the previous night. That was another one of my pastimes, and since we didn't have a television or a Playstation, I went to Graham's house. His house wasn't too far, and I would sometimes go in the evenings after making dinner. Nayeem would join us, though he wasn't really any good at computer games. They didn't have a games console at Nayeem's house either because his mum didn't allow it. She said it fried your brains out and stopped the circulation of blood from going to your head. I don't know where she got that one from, but we had a good laugh about it when Nayeem told us. We told him to wait until he was old enough to buy his own, then he could sneak it into his bedroom without his mum knowing.

School wasn't all happiness and joy for everyone. Bullies did exist and operated below the radar. Although they were small in number and you could count them on your fingers, the impact they had was massive. There was a girl called Becky who was bullied by a gang of four girls from her year group. Becky had it really tough—her parents had separated and her mum was struggling with two other younger children. The bullies picked on the way

Becky looked. Her clothes were very dirty and her hair was always tangled and scraped back with a simple elastic band. The white shirt she wore as part of the school uniform was far too small for her, had holes in it and was visibly black around the collars and cuffs. She also smelt strange—not body odour or anything like that, but a strange kind of greasy smell came from her hair and clothes if you stood too close to her. She didn't have any friends so she spent her break and lunch times in the library or in homework club.

The bullies called her all sorts of horrible names—the kind that I don't want to repeat. They even said nasty things about her dad as one of the bullies knew what happened between Becky's parents. Everyone had seen Becky's mum hang around Whitechapel market around 5:30pm on weekdays, when the market stall traders packed away anything they didn't sell and put them into boxes for the road sweepers to sweep up. Before the road sweepers took away the goods, Becky's mum and others searched through them and carefully sifted through the fruits and vegetables, which they either placed into their bags or tossed to one side. You can only imagine the kind of 'ammunition' the bullies got when they saw Becky's mum foraging around for leftover food. One of the girls took a picture on her phone and sent it around to everyone at school.

I always stuck up for Becky. Of course, the bullies called me names too like 'Becky's boyfriend' or 'Becky's bodyguard'. It didn't bother me, though. She was always grateful when I stood up for her.

"You didn't have to do that," she would say, wiping away her tears. "I try to ignore them, you know, try not to let them bother me, but they just keep coming." Becky was a soft target—she didn't have any friends, no one to stick up for her and even the teachers couldn't keep up with all the bullies and name-callers.

"One of these days, I'm gonna hurt one them girls really bad and get myself kicked out," she would say.

"Don't be stupid. That's exactly what they want. You keep your head down and get on with it," I told her. I couldn't always be there for her and she certainly couldn't help when Razor and his crew picked on me. I found strength in helping Becky because I knew how vulnerable she was, but there was no one to look out for me. Razor's lot always picked on me in lessons, during break and lunch times and even on my way to and from school if I was unlucky enough to bump into him and his hooligans. Razor had links to the street boys and thought he was untouchable. They picked on me for the clothes I wore, which were too small, too big, or too tattered and they picked on me for being skinny, which made me look physically weak like I couldn't hold myself in a fight. He called me 'pretty boy' for brushing my hair neatly to one side rather than spiked up like theirs. I always tried to dodge them and not let their words affect me, but deep down it did. At times I really wanted to punch Razor in the nose, hear it crack and feel his warm blood all over my knuckles. He definitely deserved it. But I knew I couldn't do that.

School was also full of other interesting and strange people. I found the 'Cookie Dealers' really cool—they were a network of students, who, like me, came from families that were struggling to get by. But these guys didn't settle and accept their situation. Instead they rivalled the overpriced school canteen and started selling big cookies during break and lunch times. They had a team of students who waited for packets of large cookies to be marked down in price in all the local supermarkets and then purchased around twenty to thirty packets of these cookies, with each packet containing about five to six large cookies. They had all types: chocolate chip cookies, white chocolate cookies, raspberry cookies and plain cookies. They brought these packets for about twenty-five pence per pack, which contained five cookies and then sold each cookie for fifty pence (the school canteen cookies cost sixty-five pence). The canteen recently raised their prices on everything to help make up for the shortfall caused by cuts to their budget. So naturally everyone bought off the Cookie Dealers, who were turning over a good profit every day. They were very secretive and no one really knew who the main students were, but I heard they were making fifty to sixty pounds each per week and the school was none the wiser about what was going on. I observed them selling in teams of two or three, with one always keeping a lookout. They had a good system—it worked brilliantly. I couldn't help but admire their organisation and determination. I wondered if some of the teachers were also part of their network since they always complained about their pay.

For me, school, friends and computer games were all my much-needed escape from reality. But when those things came to an end for the day (or the evening), I always felt a terrible lump in my throat because I knew that the 'escape' was over and I was going back to face the music. It was like I was trying to escape prison every night, except I never made it out to go on the run like they did in the Prison Break series, but got found out by the warden and the prison guards who threw me back into my cell.

On one evening walking back from Graham's, I felt the temperature drop and heard the faint howling sounds of the wind and the rustling newspapers blowing in the air. I saw Riya standing outside the Post Office. I watched as she untied her hair to fix her clips and then tied it back again with a red hairband. She gave me a wave and a smile as soon as she spotted me. I walked towards her. I noticed the hairband didn't make a difference in her fight against the oncoming wind—she still had a few hairs covering her face and those light brown, gazelle eyes of hers. She looked up at me like she was trying to read my face.

"What's up, how's school? You thought about which Sixth Form or College you want to go to next year?" she asked. Her voice was like warm butter and I got a whiff of the strawberry shampoo she used in her hair. I tried not to stand too close.

"Sixth Form?" I replied, still half shy and hesitant. I was completely caught off guard. "I'm just trying to focus on getting through my final exams this year."

"I know, but you have to start thinking about next year, you know? Otherwise you won't get into where you want."

"I'll probably stay on at my current school to be honest," I told her. "Their Sixth Form isn't too bad. I know all the teachers and I'm not too picky. I just don't know what to apply for yet."

"Yeah, Sixth Form at your school is alright. It's actually one of my choices—I've already applied! My dad wants me to stay close and it's one of the closest."

"Typical Riya," I said, laughing. "You haven't changed much."

"What do you mean?" she asked, smiling back at me and blushing.

"I mean you were always well ahead of everyone at primary school. You were so organised and always knew what you wanted to do. It's really good. I wish I could plan ahead like you!"

"Nah, I'm not really," she responded, trying to be modest. "I just make it seem that way. Anyway, do you know how many times I've waved at you before but you just didn't see me? I'm surprised you even saw me now."

"Seriously? I didn't mean to blank you. I would have waved back if I saw you."

"No, it's fine. I knew you didn't see me. I sometimes see you walking to school—you're always lost in your thoughts like Aristotle!"

"Really? When did you see me? I didn't even notice!"

"Yeah, obviously you didn't notice, you were in a different world! Are you sure you're okay?"

"I'm fine, honestly, just the usual stuff, you know. Mock exams coming up, coursework deadlines and other stuff," I said, trying to sound convincing.

"Okay, cool. Well, I gotta go." She walked off, battling against the wind, which started to blow stronger. I watched her walk away. I wanted her to stay. I wanted to speak to her, tell her about my problems. She seemed like such a warm, understanding person. Even if she couldn't help, I still wanted to open up to her. "Turn around," I whispered to myself and she did—only slightly as she crossed the road. Our eyes met, and she smiled and waved again. I exhaled and thought again about how nice her hair smelt. I shook my head. I needed to keep my distance. I knew I wasn't allowed to have female friends. Mum would be so upset if I ever did, let alone have a girl-friend. I knew I had to be wary about how much I spoke to Riya, even though my heart told me otherwise!

* * *

Musa recommended that I start jogging with him on some evenings and do a few gym sessions in the unused basement of the mosque.

"It will help you de-stress," he said, "take your mind off things and make you feel refreshed. I think everything is getting you down. You need to break up your routine a little—do something different, work up a sweat! You know what I'm saying? And anyway, with that neatly combed hair and natural good looks mashallah, that tiny frame of yours could do with some work. We need to bulk you up a little," he laughed.

We started by jogging Tuesdays and Thursdays with one gym session on Wednesdays after isha prayer. We jogged around the outer rim of Crescent Park, which was approximately two and a half miles. The first time was tough—not only did I work up a sweat by the end, but my heart was pounding like it was going to rip out of my chest. And that wasn't the worst part! I struggled to get out of bed the next morning because my muscles were so sore. Musa didn't struggle at all, but for him I guess it must have felt like a short stride. The second time was slightly easier and by the third week I actually started to enjoy it. My lungs absorbed the fresh air and I enjoyed running around the park and taking in its beautiful scenery: the perfectly arranged flower beds in the Rose

Garden, the small waterfall, the different sized blue and yellow paddling boats and the brown and green benches that sat symmetrically beside the part where people usually fed the ducks. I noticed everything as we jogged at a steady pace around the park, which was always lit up by soft lamp lights. While my body worked hard to keep up with Musa's pace, my mind switched off. Nothing really mattered when I was out there, not even the bitter cold. I came home, showered, offered my salaah and had a perfect night's sleep.

I told Musa about Razor and his crew. "People who are already working for the street boys have got no future. They're going down in life and probably wanna take as many people down with them as possible."

"I know, but they just won't leave me alone."

"Is it just you they pick on?"

"No, it's not just me. They pick on anyone really, as long as they think they can get away with it."

"Listen, Nadim, inform your teachers and just ignore them. If you want I can pick you up from school now and then and drive you home so they don't bother you after school?"

"Come on, Musa, I can't ask you to do that. You wake up really early for work and you probably want to be sleeping in the afternoons."

"Look, it's really no bother. Let me know."

"Yeah, but it won't solve the problem, will it? They'll still be there when you're not there! Sometimes, I swear to God, I just want to punch one of them right in the nose," I said, gritting my teeth and clenching my fists.

"Alright, calm down! You don't wanna be getting into fights, Nadim, you'll get kicked out of school and then you'll have nothing better to do than join Razor's pay-masters. Look, I don't want you to be fighting, but if it ever came to it, all you need to know is how to defend yourself. I used to do a bit of kick-boxing when I was a lot younger. I kept it up, but I need a training partner. Are you up for it?"

"Wow, yeah, I'd love to! I used to do a bit of kick-boxing when I was in Year Five as well. Dad used to take me and Nabil on Tuesdays. It was only for a short while though."

"Great! So you've done a bit of martial arts already! They've got some gear in the mosque basement. You help me with the mitts and the punch bags and I'll show you how to throw some deadly punches and kicks and how to use your knees, elbows and head."

"Serious? That'd be awesome! Can't wait!"

The jogging, the gym sessions and the kick-boxing classes helped me to find myself again, after everything that was going wrong. I couldn't always make the jogging sessions with Musa because of homework, but I never missed the gym and kick-boxing sessions.

"Remember," he said, looking at me intently, "I don't ever wanna hear you getting into a fight in school. That's not why we're doing this. It's only for your fitness, confidence and if you ever need to defend yourself!"

"Alright," I laughed, "don't worry. I'm not going to go around hurting anybody."

Chapter 11

The Visits

We tried to visit Nabil as often as we could. He was being held at a Young Offender Institution in Swindon, which took us two hours to get to by train from Marylebone. We would have visited more often, but the cost of the train tickets meant we couldn't. Even the £10 Mum sent him every month was a struggle.

The regime of the visits was particularly difficult and draining for Mum. We got the underground to Marylebone station, and then caught another overground train to Swindon, after which we had to walk for ages. That was followed by a waiting system, which was pretty much on a 'first come, first serve' basis even though Nabil sent us a Visiting Order (VO) weeks beforehand. When they called us, the prison staff checked our VO against our ID. Then they told us to leave all of our possessions inside the flimsy lockers that didn't close properly in the visitors' area and proceed to the visiting centre where everyone was searched from head to toe by strange-looking people wearing blue rubber gloves. We then joined a second queue for the prison dog to smell us (I think this was to sniff out drugs that were being smuggled in). Not that it worked—criminals found lots of creative ways to smuggle things in using whatever method they could. Last week there was a story on the news about someone trying to smuggle in mobile phones and drugs using a remote-controlled drone!

After all the searches were complete, we were taken into a very dull, bleak room where the chairs and tables were bolted to the ground. They tried to make the place appear friendly and welcoming by painting it with brightly coloured children's wall drawings, but it didn't work. It was still a prison. The whole ordeal of the journey, the wait and the intrusive searches was sometimes too much for Mum. She was in constant dhikr the whole time, and in tears even before our actual visit started. We went to our allocated table before Nabil was brought in with just enough time for Mum to wipe away her tears and compose herself.

The visits were mostly pleasant, until it was time to say goodbye. They were supposed to last for two hours, but felt like ten minutes. We talked about anything and everything. Nabil tried to put on a brave face and always said how easy he was finding things inside. He seemed to have learnt from everything that happened to him and appeared focused on improving himself.

"Things are good, Mum," he said. "They put me on all these courses and I'm really enjoying the Electrical Engineering one. If I complete it, I could get a job with a big utility company! I hit the gym three days a week, have classes almost every day, two days of drugs counselling and anger management, and the rest of the time I get to socialise and call home," he continued with renewed enthusiasm. "I'm staying out of trouble and keeping my head down so I should be home before the end of next year if I'm lucky—with 'good behaviour' and that."

As he spoke, Mum seemed to be soothed by the knowledge that Nabil was coping well with his situation. It meant that she had one less thing to worry about. Nabil knew that so he just kept filling her head with his fantasy description of prison. The reality was that the entire prison system was at breaking point and there were constant fights, riots and even deaths. But Nabil never talked about that during the visits, or how much he was missing everyone.

He didn't tell Mum, for example, that it took him over six months to settle in. In that time, he was attacked, had things stolen from him and even spent two weeks in solitary confinement for trying to stop a fight! He also didn't tell Mum that he cried himself to sleep every night because he hated being away from his family. No, those things he only mentioned to me in his letters or when he spoke to me on the phone. He wrote individual, personalised letters to everyone, trying from a distance to be the big brother we all needed.

Salaams,

To my little brother Nadim,

I hope this letter finds you in the best of health and the highest of imaan. Alhamdulillah, everything's alright from my end. I've started praying regularly and met some really good brothers here. They're helping me to stay out of trouble and stay safe when things get tough.

Sometimes I get really anxious and feel guilty when I think about you guys. You know how sorry I am for everything I've put you through. I should've been there for you and I'm so sorry that I haven't been the big brother I should have been. I feel so guilty and ashamed for letting things get the way they did, but I've changed—I promise. I've learned from my mistakes and I'm trying to fix my ways.

Please forgive me. I'm so proud of you and I'm sure Dad would be too if he was here. You remind me of him so much. Keep doing what you're doing, man. Take good care of Mum and the twins and don't forget to take care of yourself.

Be strong, bro. Inshallah I'll be back soon and we can make up for lost time.

Wasalaam,

Your big brother Nabz

I read his letters over and over again. I read them in his voice each time because although I never told him, I did miss him a lot.

I didn't understand how Nabil got there. He was so intelligent, bright and articulate and all the teachers always said he had a great future ahead of him on parents' evenings. He was so confident and guided me when I had a problem. I remember the time I borrowed his bike and went too fast down the slope leading down to the Regent's Canal footpath. I didn't turn left quickly enough and hit the wall in front of me. The force completely threw me forward. I came off the bike and landed on top of the benches in front of the wall. The bike was completely gone! The handle bar came off and the front bar that held the handle bar up snapped in half. I was expecting Nabil to completely flip, but he didn't. Instead he ran to me, helped me up and walked me home. The bike was irreparable so we left it there. He didn't say anything, but I could tell he was upset—it was the first bike Dad had bought for him. As we were walking home, after a long silence, he muttered, "It's just a bike. Dad will buy me another one. We can't buy another one of you though, can we?" We both smiled.

That kind and considerate person slowly started to change as he got older. He started to care more about his self-image and how people perceived him. He started lifting weights, bulking up, smoking and getting into fights at school. He started hanging around with the wrong sorts of boys—the street boys. No one messed with those guys because everyone knew what they were capable of. They went around the school acting like they owned it. I think Nabil admired the way people feared them, the way they managed to get away with so much and the mystery that surrounded them. Nabil even started to forge notes to bunk off school. That's when Dad finally caught him. He promised to change his ways and sort himself out and he did for a while, but when Dad got ill, Nabil turned back to his old ways again and this time, to a point of no return.

When the visits ended, Mum got very emotional. She tried to compose herself and remain dignified, but sometimes giant sobs would escape her. I guess it was even more painful with Nabil being the eldest. She probably thought she could rely on him after Dad passed away.

The journey back was always very silent. Mum would barely utter a word. She wouldn't eat either. When we reached home, she would have a cup of tea, take her medication and go straight to sleep.

I knew Nabil had messed up but I found it hard to see him in prison. Sometimes I didn't even want to talk to him when he called every week because it was so difficult. I just gave him my salaams and passed it over to Mum.

He probably thought something was up but never pressed me to tell him what. He knew we all had problems and challenges that we were dealing with in our own way. I felt my heart was being pulled in so many different directions. Part of me loved him and missed him, and the other part of me hated him for being in prison when he should have been here, with us.

One evening after our monthly visit, I left Mum sleeping and put the twins to bed after giving them sandwiches for dinner—I didn't have the energy to make anything else. Graham and Hisham came over. They knew the days of the visits were always difficult. On those days, I didn't really want to socialise and I definitely wasn't in the mood for entertaining my friends. After watching the football highlights on Graham's phone, using his usual sense of humour, he tried to cheer me up.

"Hey Nadim," he said with a cheeky grin on his face, "you should have seen Ridwan in Drama today... he tried to pull off one of his roundhouse kicks and ended up kicking that girl Nicola in the chest. He almost knocked her unconscious! We all burst out laughing cos she ran after him like she was gonna thump him! You should have been there, man!"

"Yeah, it was proper funny," added Hisham, trying to contain himself, "imagine if she fainted. He would've had to give her mouth to mouth to revive her!"

"I'm sure she would have loved that—cute little Ridwan trying to breathe life back into her," laughed Graham, looking at me for a reaction.

"Yeah, I'm sure it was funny, guys," I said plainly. "I'm just so tired, man. It's been a long day."

"Yeah we know, mate, just trying to crack you up a little," Hisham said. He stopped, probably realising that I wasn't in the mood for jokes. "Look, bro," he added, "I know it must be tough man, but hold tight... not long now... Nabil will be back soon inshallah and you'll all be together again."

"Yeah, man, not long to go..." added Graham. "You'll look back at this in a few years' time and be surprised at how quickly the time passed."

"Thanks, guys," I replied. "It's just... things just feel so tough sometimes, like there's no end." I took a deep breath. I really didn't want to speak anymore. "Anyway, I'm really tired. I'm going to try and get some sleep. I'll catch you guys in school on Monday."

They both got up, grabbed their coats and left. I was grateful for having friends like them but the truth is, I couldn't really open up to them. I didn't know how to and to be honest, I didn't really want to. I knew I needed to talk to someone and not bottle everything up inside, but who did I really have? Musa was a good friend, but I couldn't tell him everything. I didn't know if he would understand. I thought of Riya, but even she was off limits. I was breaking up inside, cracking up into small, thin pieces. I knew I needed to pull myself together and stay strong. But some days were just too difficult. It was too much—too much to bear, too much to shoulder and too much to withstand. Only Allah knows how close I was to having a complete breakdown. The only thing that kept me together was Mum and the twins. I didn't want to let them down—I couldn't. I knew how helpless they would be without me.

Chapter 12

New Hope?

It was unusually cold for a spring evening with a brutal wind roaring through the city streets. As I was being thrust forward through the long road leading up to our estate, the winds would appear to momentarily calm before projecting more vicious, punishing icy blasts. The trees were trying to stubbornly hold their ground against the onslaught. The stars on that evening were particularly luminous. The bright crescent moon remained both with me as a companion and above me as a guide and mentor throughout my journey home. Pondering over the beauty of the natural creation made me wonder about the magnificence of the Creator. I tried to always have hope in Allah and belief in Him. If I didn't, I knew I'd fall through the cracks and keep falling to no end.

I was lost in these thoughts when I saw Mr Cooper hurrying towards me.

"Hi there, Mr Cooper," I called out in a slightly raised voice, waving my hand. I thought he wouldn't hear me over the howling wind.

"Hi there, young man!" he said. "Hope you enjoyed those sweet potato chips last week." I had taken them from the Community Fridge last Friday—they were a rare treat and reminded me of Dad. He used to make them for us on his days off work alongside homemade bean burger wraps. Mum said they were much too expensive to buy, so when I saw a small bag in the Community Fridge, my hand naturally reached for them.

"Yes, they were lovely, Mr Cooper, thank you."

"Oh that's quite alright, young man, I'm glad you enjoyed them. Things like that don't stay in the fridge for long, I tell you. You were very lucky! Anyway, I must be on my way now. I've closed the shop a bit early today because the heating and hot water are down. There's another water leak at the end of the street—can you believe it?! Anyway, say hello to your mum for me," he shouted, clutching his hat and coat as the wind almost threw him off balance.

"Alright, Mr Cooper, thanks again!"

The thought of Dad's sweet potato chips stayed in my mind. I could almost smell and taste them, and see Dad getting lost in 'organised chaos' in the kitchen as he ran around trying to perfect his masterpiece. He was like an eccentric artist, creating a huge mess with all his ingredients and cooking equipment before presenting his very finely cooked dish, which sat perfectly on a plate with well-proportioned sides, salad and dressing. If you looked at the amazing end product, you'd never think it was born out of so much chaos.

All of a sudden, I could hear a loud ringing sound in the distance, gradually getting closer. Police sirens. The intrusive noise shattered the tranquil thoughts that I was enjoying. I sped up, deciding to take a shortcut through the communal garden near our estate. The roaring engines of the two cars and their deafening sirens were getting closer and closer, as well as the sound of hurried footsteps behind me. Before I could turn around, a dark figure in all black shot past me. I felt his right arm brush against my left shoulder, nearly knocking me off balance, as he dodged the obstacles in his pathway like a missile with a homing device trying to reach its target. I heard him panting heavily, running like his life depended on it.

He ground to a halt, the wide, tall trees providing him with the perfect cover. I saw him reach for the inside of his jacket. He slipped out a small bag. I watched as it landed in a pile of dead, soggy leaves. Before I could blink, he was gone.

A third police car was waiting at the end of the street, not far from our block. It was no use. Out of breath and out of ideas, the shadowy figure placed his hands on top of the white, marked police car. Things like this weren't very common in my local area, but they weren't exactly rare either. Seriously though, three police cars just to catch one man? They took ages to come on the night we were burgled, and told us they were over-stretched and under-resourced! I thought, shaking my head.

Onlookers had already begun to mill around, watching the drama unfold and whispering to one another. I hung back from the crowd, shifting from one foot to another, my mind casting back to what only I had witnessed a few moments ago. *Seven trees*, said a small voice in my head. That's how far I was. No, I thought. I can't. I shouldn't. All of the police cars had pulled up now. The crowd was growing, shielding me from view. *Just seven trees away*, the voice sang. Before I realised what was happening, my legs began to pull me backwards, my heart beating faster and faster, each step becoming slower and heavier. *I'll just go home.* But I didn't. I couldn't. The curiosity, the mystery and the absurdity of the whole situation pulled

101

me towards it like a powerful magnet. I was three trees away. Two trees. One. I quickly glanced around to see if anyone was looking and then kneeled down. I couldn't see anything. The shadow of the tree and the darkness of the night meant I had to feel around the bottom of the tree like a blind man. By this time my heart was racing so much that droplets of sweat began to trickle down the centre of my forehead.

After a few frantic jabs, I felt something smooth graze my trembling hands. It was slightly heavy, half-visible and half-obscured by the night. I moved it up to my face. I got a strong whiff of leather. What now? What do I do with it? It wasn't mine. It wasn't my problem. I should have left it there. Only I didn't. I was amazed at how cool-ly and calmly I picked it up, undid the zip of my jacket, and placed it under my arm, clutching it tightly between my elbow and rib cage. My next thought: *Run.* I ran home as quickly as I could, my mind racing. Why would some-one on the run from the police dump a bag where no one could see it? What was he trying to hide? Why did I pick it up? Maybe the police will be looking for it. Did I just in-terfere with a police matter? What would they do if they found out? Thoughts buzzed around my mind for what seemed like an eternity before I reached our tower block.

The faded dark yellow paint in the staircase and the grey plain concrete steps seemed to be never-ending. The dull, clashing colours overpowered me. I always found our tower block harsh and unsettling to look at, but now it was just amplified. Approaching our front door, I threw myself in and quickly ran up to my bedroom. I tossed the bag under my bed, collapsing on top of the mattress. I tried my best to steady my breathing. I didn't have time to process what had just happened. I needed to fix dinner for Mum and the twins first before I did anything else. I knew they were waiting for me.

I kept forgetting about the bag during dinner, but then the memory would hit me again and set my heart racing. After giving Mum her medication, we all settled down for her to carry on with the next chapter of our evening reading. We were reading *Oliver Twist*. She began reading out the scene where Fagin, the 'loathsome reptile' tries to convince Oliver to steal for him.

"Ewww, he's horrible, Mum! He's so ugly!" Nusaybah exclaimed. Nabeela squealed in agreement.

"It's his actions that are ugly, sweetheart. He's been a thief all his life and committed bad actions that Allah forbids us to do."

I felt Mum's words like a slap in the face. What were the odds of her reading out that scene at that exact moment? Was it a sign from Allah that I had done something terrible? The thought of the black bag suddenly churned my stomach again. I had stolen, but I didn't even know what. I knew I had to look inside, but I couldn't bring myself to.

I got up, took a deep breath and began to walk to my bedroom, which was only a few steps away. But as soon as I left the living room, every step seemed difficult as I battled and struggled with the thought of what I might find inside that bag. It seemed like time suddenly slowed down and with each step I took a new breath. I felt the thinning, old carpet under my feet, stopped and paused for a moment before progressing on to the next. Finally, I reached my room, and swung the door open. Whatever it was, I had to face it. I wasn't going to let it torture me anymore. I dived towards the bottom of my bed like an Olympic swimmer. I placed both of my trembling hands on the mouth of the black leather bag, opening its jaw as wide as I could, ready for it to swallow me up.

* * *

I didn't know what to feel! A combination of happiness and shock paralysed me. Tears ran down my eyes and I cried a few gentle sobs of relief. Was this it? Was this what I had been waiting for?

I heard footsteps coming towards my bedroom door. Mum knocked. "Are you okay, Nadim?" she asked in a low, faint voice. I quickly covered everything up with my duvet and opened the door, but only slightly.

"I'm fine, Mum," I said. "What's up? How far have you guys got up to with *Oliver Twist*?"

"Just finished the chapter we were on, darling. Why didn't you stay? You got up and left. I was hoping you could take over the reading."

"I was going to, Mum, but I'm really tired tonight and wanted to get an early night."

"Alright, darling. Are you sure you're okay? You just seemed a bit... not yourself, really."

"I'm fine, Mum," I reassured her. "It's nothing, really." I was relieved that she didn't enquire any further. I didn't want to let her in. She had enough of her own troubles without me offloading and burdening her with the chaos and turmoil that I was feeling. Mum knew us all very well and picked up on it if we ever acted out of the ordinary. She probably guessed that I was worried about something, but she didn't press me any further. That's how she was even when she had a million and one things to worry about herself—she always looked out for us and checked if we were all okay. She never forced anything out of us, but listened and tried to find solutions if we explained our problems to her.

"Okay, well, if you need anything, I'll be in my room." I heard her footsteps slowly fade away.

I locked my door shut and turned the duvet over. My feelings were indescribable. But I held myself together. I couldn't scream. I couldn't cry. I just sat there taking it all in. After a while my racing heart and churning stomach settled. I couldn't decide if I was going to tell anyone or what I wanted do with all those new, shiny Bank of England notes. Had I become accidentally rich?

Chapter 13

Money Talks

I spent most of the night holding those bundles in my hand. What bundles of joy they were! I couldn't believe my eyes. I took them out of their plastic packets and ripped off the elastic bands that bound them. £25,000 in total. Ten bundles of £2,500 made up of £20 notes. I counted the whole thing twice. It was definitely £25,000!

What could I do with all that money? I couldn't take it to the bank—they'd get suspicious and probably think that I was part of some drug cartel. This must be a gift from Allah for all the hardships my family and I were facing. It would alter our lives completely. No more tightening our belts. No more watching every penny. This could be a new beginning for all of us, where we weren't frightened to open the mail just in case it was another bill, where we could go back to eating what we wanted and wearing what everyone else was wearing, where we didn't have to be embarrassed because we couldn't afford the already subsidised contribution towards the school trip. No. No, sir! No more!

The first thing I was going to do was pay off that horrible gas bill. I wouldn't even bother fighting them to tell them it was their fault the bill was so high in the first place. Nope! I'd just pay them off and save myself the hassle... then I would buy everyone some new clothes from the high street. No more Mell Street Market! Then I would fill up the fridge and cupboards with endless types of different foods like we used to have when Dad was around... no more soup or sandwiches for dinner! After that I'd buy a 50-inch flat screen smart TV and the latest PlayStation console with all the best games. I'd then buy the latest smartphones for everyone—no more cheap, basic phones without any credit just to use for emergencies. Towards the end of the year when I'd finished all my exams, I'd book a holiday somewhere in a hot country, a 5-star all-inclusive holiday, and oh yeah, we'd fly first class because after all this, I think we deserved it.

Out of my gratefulness I decided I'd donate some money to the local food bank so others could also enjoy some decent food. After all that, I'd still have money for the internet, Sky and the home alarm system to be paid for the whole year. I could even install security cameras to frighten those nasty burglars away.

But what then...? After the beautiful scenes I was dreaming in my head came to an end, it finally dawned on me... what then? After spending all of that money that wasn't really mine (I'd done nothing to deserve it), what would I do then? Would it really solve all my problems? Yes, for the time being, but what then? Slowly, the reality of the situation kicked in. And the reality was this: this was money that was thrown away by someone who was on the run from the police. It must be money made from selling drugs or stolen goods, otherwise why would he dump it like that? Why did he try to hide it? It didn't make sense. Now that it was in my hands, what did that make me? A criminal? An accomplice?

I was in possession of 'dirty' money that wasn't mine! The thought weighed heavy on my heart... what had I done? Why didn't I just leave it where I found it? And now that I did have it, what should I do with it? Put it back where I found it? Maybe that would help the people behind it. Maybe the place where he dumped it was a known spot for them. So I couldn't do that. Then what could I do? Hand it to the police? They might think I was involved in one way or another. In fact, by picking it up and holding on to it, I already was involved. I could spend it all and never think about it again, but that wouldn't be right. I wouldn't feel comfortable spending that money. Anything I bought with that money would be void of any blessing and even if I gave it away in charity, it wouldn't be accepted by Allah.

The thoughts invaded my mind again. What have I done and what am I to do now? I let myself down. Let my family down. Let down my Lord, the One who created me and cared for me my whole life. Why did I pick up that bag? Not only did I open up the possibility of being arrested for possessing the money, but I also put myself and my family at risk of harm from criminals who could be looking for this money. I was petrified! The guilt began to gnaw away at me. I'd never done anything so reckless in my whole life. How could I be so stupid?

* * *

When Wednesday came around again, I didn't want to go to the mosque, the gym or have a kick-boxing session with Musa. My mind was all over the place. I just wanted to stay at home and lock myself away from everyone, but I knew I couldn't hide from Musa. He would come looking for me and then ask a thousand and one questions. I reluctantly went but I found my mind couldn't focus on the prayer. I just completed it without any concentration like a programmed robot. Once the gym session was over I ploughed through the circuit training Musa planned for us, working on my jabs, right hooks and defensive posture.

"Jab, jab, then follow through, right punch, and then back off with guards right up," shouted Musa with pads on both hands, ready to receive my punches. "And again," he yelled, this time throwing back a left swing and a right swing for me to duck from. "Keep those guards up, never drop them!"

I was doing fine as Musa moved around the room, coming at me from a different direction each time. I was getting into the rhythm. I felt my punches getting stronger and more accurate, but then just as I started to forget about those bundles of money that sat underneath my bed, the image of the bag, the money and the strange guy who dropped it under the tree came flashing back right in front of my eyes. For a moment, a split second, I lost concentration and suddenly, I felt two consecutive thuds and the sound of Musa's hissing as the mitts made contact with my right and left cheek. I saw what looked like a bright light each time the mitts connected to my cheeks. I went crashing down on the mat.

"Nadim, you alright, bro?!" Musa threw off his mitts and rushed towards the ground. I opened my eyes to find his big wide eyes staring back at me. I blinked several times, staring blankly.

"Yeah, I'll be alright," I replied, still dizzy. "Just give me a second."

"I didn't mean to hit you hard, bro. I'm really sorry, man," he said, looking guilty. "Damn!"

"It's okay, I'm fine. Just lost concentration for a bit. Do you mind if we stop for now? I'm a bit knackered today."

"Of course not, bro. You get changed and we'll walk back together." He was still shaking his head and looked very disappointed with himself. "I'm really sorry, man. I hope I didn't hurt you."

"No, Musa, don't be silly. I'm fine, you just caught me off guard that's all. Don't get happy, yeah—your punches weren't that fast," I joked, rubbing my face and eyes.

"Those weren't punches, mate, just little hooks to get you moving and learn to keep your guard up. If one of my punches landed on you, I'd have had to carry you home, trust me," he grinned.

The night was still young. We walked back slowly through the familiar leafy pathway that led back to our estate. We saw a herd of the street boys milling around in the street. There was one who was much younger than the rest of them. One of the older boys offered him a cigarette. He refused at first, but then reluctantly took it between his thumb and index finger. He took it close to his mouth, took a small drag and breathed in. The end lit up and glowed red like a torch as the paper burned bright. The young boy looked uncomfortable, and the harsh smoke must have hit his throat like a bullet because tears quickly sprang from his eyes and he was unable to contain the violent cough that broke out wildly from his chest. He gave the cigarette back, wheezing and coughing uncontrollably. The older boys cheered and roared with laughter, slapping him on his back.

"Now you're one of us," growled a tall, bulky figure. "Whenever we call, you answer, y'get me? Then you mans will be given your missions, y'understand?" The young boy nodded in agreement. "There's a lot of cash to be made yeah, but we all start small," he continued, handing the younger boy what looked like a five or ten pound note.

This must be how they get initiated, I thought to myself: smoke and then start your 'first mission' to earn some money. These street boys took advantage of youngsters who came from poor families and used them to do their dirty work, transporting drugs and stolen goods from one place to another for a few pounds here and there. All of that for money.... I shook my head. The bag! I briefly forgot about the bag crammed full of notes in my room. Then I realised that my problem had just gotten bigger. The bag must somehow belong to one of the street boys. The dark figure who ran past me that night was almost definitely one of them. Great, I muttered to myself sarcastically. I tried so hard to steer well clear of those guys, and now I actually had something that belonged to one of them! What am I going to do next? How was I going to get myself out of this one? I didn't say anything to Musa. How could I? We just carried on walking.

I saw him shaking his head in disapproval. "That's child exploitation right there," he said, raising his voice and pointing right at them. They saw him too. He wasn't scared of them. They must have known who he was. "Trust me, you don't wanna end up linked to them no matter how desperate your situation is." We both walked on and climbed up the stairs to our flats.

Too late, I thought.

Chapter 14

Mopeds

" **A**fter a string of robberies by a highly organised moped gang, the Metropolitan Police believe they have finally made a breakthrough. The main members of the so-called Masked Manz gang, who are believed to be responsible for a string of robberies throughout East London, have been arrested this evening and are currently in police custody waiting to be questioned. Police are appealing to the local community in Mile End to come forward as they are trying to piece together intelligence regarding this highly organised and highly sophisticated team of robbers, who have been linked to numerous home robberies over the past year."

I watched the six o'clock news in Graham's house that evening with a huge lump in my throat and an unsettling, churning feeling in the pit of my stomach. It felt like there was a big, slimy creature swimming in my stomach. I didn't say anything to him. I just sat there, empty and quiet.

"What's up, Nadim?" he asked. "You're just staring at the TV. I didn't know the news was that interesting."

"It's nothing, man," I told him. "I'm just a little tired. Didn't sleep properly last night."

"Sleeping is my hobby! If only there was a job where they paid you to sleep."

"Yeah, that would be your dream job."

"Yeah, dream job, where all I'd be doing is dreaming," he laughed.

"Anyway, I have to go." I got up, putting on my coat. I wanted to tell Graham about the bag, the money and all of my worries, but I couldn't. I left and took the short walk home. Walking through our estate, I saw the ripped daffodils on the flower bed that I passed every day. The kids on the estate always did things like that—that's probably why the council stopped taking care of it. All of the flowers were decayed and dead, and the flower beds were strewn with empty drink cans and cigarette buds.

The enormity of the whole situation weighed heavily on my chest. I kept on asking myself: what have I done? Now the police were appealing for witnesses and information. What should I do? I knew what a difference this money could make to our lives, but I knew it was wrong to even keep it, let alone spend it. The money must belong to this Masked Manz gang who somehow had links to the local street boys in our area. It sounded like a complex web I had no way of understanding. The arrest I witnessed a few days ago must have led to other arrests and now the police were appealing for help!

At school, at home and at the mosque, wherever I turned, I couldn't find solace. As I sat in our weekly assembly at school, the Headteacher kept on repeating: "Be the best you can be. That's all we can expect from you."

But was I really doing it? Was I being the best I could be? On the one hand, yes, I was proud of looking after and looking out for everyone including myself. That wasn't easy. I had to grow up really quickly to cope and in some ways I probably skipped a lot of my childhood to serve my family. But on the other hand, I was holding on to something that wasn't mine.

Nothing weighed on my mind more than this guilt. Maybe I was the missing piece of the puzzle that could help the police put these guys away for good and break up the operations of the street boys. Maybe I was holding crucial information that was holding back the police investigations. After all, if they didn't have evidence of any stolen goods how could they charge anyone?

The guilt turned to emotional turmoil and then panic. The anxiety almost turned to agony as I constantly thought of the worst: what if police officers came storming through my door and arrested me for holding this 'evidence'? What would happen to Mum? The twins? That's what it became at that point. Not hope, not a blessing, and definitely not the answer to my problems.

As news of the infamous Masked Manz gang unfolded all over the local newspapers and television, I couldn't escape it. It was everywhere. Everyone was talking about it—my friends at school and even my English teacher Mr Read (who always used current events as a way of teaching texts) spoke about them.

"Such is the influence of Dickens from our English literary heritage," he said in his posh voice, "that even highly organised criminal gangs in our time operate similarly to how pickpockets operated in his novel *Oliver Twist*."

A strange comparison, I thought, but that was Mr Read for you—always trying to bring things down to our level, even things that seemed so far-fetched. Fagin from *Oliver Twist* organised pickpockets, whereas this moped gang broke into peoples' houses, mugged people on the street and used street boys as part of their wide network. They did share some similarities I guess, except Fagin wasn't real, and unfortunately these guys were!

I didn't want anything to remind me. I wanted to escape from all of it, but there was nowhere to go. I couldn't get rid of the bag. I had already touched the bag and the money. The police could catch up with me using their forensic teams to link me to the money like they do in CSI. I was stuck. What could I do? I had money that I couldn't spend and I couldn't get rid of.

I found myself drifting off in class... I saw the street boys surrounding my home, armed with sticks, baseball bats and knives. They were at the bottom of our block, before walking up the staircase, through our door and into my bedroom. I only woke up when I felt Mr Read's finger poke me in the back as he circulated the classroom.

I couldn't remember the last time I had felt so low. I worked so hard on being the best I could be, to do right by my mum and the twins, to support my family and not let them down, and now I was so disappointed with myself.

When I got home, I was exhausted. I took the lift. They must have repaired it recently, but it was still very unpleasant. Someone had left a white, single bed mattress with visible yellow stains inside the lift. I could smell something foul coming from the mattress, so I kicked it towards the back of the lift so it didn't fall on me, but some of the yellow stains touched the tip of my trainers. I was disgusted—not sure whether it was urine, alcohol or something else, and not sure which one I hoped it was. Thankfully, we lived on the second floor, so the ride wasn't too long. I felt my mind starting to talk to me. I hadn't slept properly in days, so I flung myself on my bed in my uniform, wanting so badly to be able to sleep even for a few minutes.

I saw Riya in my dreams. She untied her gorgeous, glossy hair and looked at me with those light brown gazelle eyes, the colour of a walnut shell. Her pale skin with a hint of olive complemented her kind voice. She looked at me and greeted me with a smile like the bloom of the morning. "Why do you look so worried, Nadim?" she asked. Then her smile faded away, replaced with fear as the surrounding street boys started to close in on her. They were armed. She was holding the black bag. I wanted to help her, I wanted to shout, I wanted to run towards her. She began to cry, but I couldn't do anything. I was paralysed.

Eyes wide open. Sweating. Disorientated. What just happened? Was this the projection of my fears or some sinister vision of the future? I didn't know. I just didn't want it anymore. I wanted to get rid of it. How could an item I once believed was my saviour now become the bane of my very existence?

Fear and anxiety turned to anguish and for the first time in a long time, I cried. I let out giant sobs, trying hard not to let Mum hear me. I couldn't help it. I just cried and cried and cried until I could cry no more. Was I going mad? I couldn't tell the difference between my own thoughts and the anxiety invading my mind. I was in dangerous territory. I needed help before I ended up doing something even more stupid.

Enough! I thought, wiping away my tears. I washed my face and went downstairs. I had to make dinner and put on a brave face, no matter what I was going through.

Nabil called later on that evening. He spoke to me first.

"Nadim, make du'a for me, bro. Things are tough," he said. I sensed the distress in his voice. If he was asking me to make du'a and describing things as 'tough' then he really must have been finding it hard inside. That's what Nabil was usually like—always trying to downplay the situation and avoiding giving out details. Maybe something had happened, maybe he was in some sort of trouble, or maybe he was just having a really bad day? Whatever it was, I had no power to change things. I couldn't do anything to help. All I could do was raise my hands to the heavens as he requested and plead to my Lord to ease his situation.

"I'm sure you've seen the news," he continued. "They've transferred some of those guys from the Masked Manz gang into my prison. One or two of them are even on my wing. I don't wanna see those guys, bro. Some of them know me from before, y'know? Every time I tried to break away from them when I was outside they'd get nasty. I'm trying to leave all that mess behind me, but it just seems to follow me, even in here!"

"What if we tried to get you a transfer to another prison?" I suggested. I heard a deep sigh of despair.

"It's not that easy, bro. Prisons are full up everywhere. Forget the housing crisis that they keep banging on about on the news, this country's going through a prison crisis too! When these guys start rioting, the prison guards can't even control it—they just shut the whole place down for days. Then we can't leave our cells or call home. So a transfer is out of the question. Just make du'a, bro, but don't tell Mum. I don't want her to worry. I've gotta go now. Credit running out."

Worrying about Nabil added another strain on my heart. I couldn't help but worry about him. If they found out I had their bag and put the pieces together, not only would we all be in danger, but they could harm Nabil too! Any bit of worry and my brain would go into overdrive. The only way I could stop the heavy beating and pounding of my heart was by turning to Allah in du'a and listening to Qur'an. I knew I had made a grave mistake—I just needed to find a way to fix it. So after pleading to my Lord and having *tawakkul* in Him, I tried to relax my soul. I knew that every du'a is answered, and that it would be answered in the best way He saw fit though His Infinite Wisdom.

Chapter 15

Just What I Needed

Dad always said that 'a problem spoken about is a problem halved'. He was right. I knew I desperately needed to speak to someone, but who? I couldn't speak to Mum because she was so fragile. She might see the money as our saviour or the panic could send her over the edge—I didn't want that! I wanted to tell Musa, but I thought of how disappointed he would be. He was disgusted by everything the street boys did and stood for. How could I explain to him that I picked up money that belonged to a criminal gang and now the police were looking for it? I couldn't speak to my friends. The only sensible one was Nayeem, but I didn't want to burden him with this trouble. I couldn't speak to my Head of Year at school, Ms Thomas, even though she said she had an 'open door policy'. She was busy dealing with one incident or another with my year group. I always found her shouting at someone. In fact, I actually forgot what her normal voice sounded like. She was out of the question!

I couldn't speak to the Imam because he was too busy dealing with funerals, weddings and mosque politics. Besides, he was way too old to understand what I was going through. I couldn't relate to him. If he was a bit younger then maybe, but as it stood, this guy had grandchildren that were older than me.

So I turned again to Allah, raising my hands to Him and begging Him to find me a way out of this predicament. I knew that if I feared Allah, He would always find me a way out.

Even before I had completed my du'a after the zuhr salaah, a possible solution presented itself to me. I decided I wasn't going to speak to anyone—well, not directly anyway.

I thought the best way to approach this was to ask my English teacher, Mr Read. He seemed like an intelligent man who not only knew everything about English, but also seemed to know something about everything else. Mr Read tried not to speak about his personal life. Every time we asked him anything personal, he would simply answer, "That's unprofessional," but occasionally he would let things slip—accidentally, of course. You could easily put these occasional slips together to create a comprehensive picture of what Mr Read's personal life was like. I know you're not supposed to be nosy, but we students are very nosy and want to know about the personal lives of our teachers, however boring and mundane their lives may be. I guess it makes them more human in our eyes because you can easily forget when they keep talking about grades and progress that actually they are humans just like us. They probably have dreams, expectations, as well as fears and anxieties about life as we all do. They just seem to hide it pretty well and get on with teaching classes full of crazy teenagers.

I started my conversation with Mr Read after our double English lesson on Tuesday morning. I thought about it for a long time. I thought about how I would phrase my questions, covered in layers of code so he couldn't work out that I was actually asking for his advice for myself. I played out our conversation in my head and even thought about how I could tackle any questions from him just in case he started working out the real situation.

"Sir, I feel really sorry for Bob Cratchit. I mean he tries so hard to provide for his family and get by on the very little that Scrooge pays him," I said. "Sir, wouldn't it be nice if he suddenly found some money and became accidentally rich? He would be so fortunate."

"I'm sure we all wish we found some wealth from somewhere and became affluent by chance," he said. "But we know life doesn't work like that."

"But sir, suppose he did find some money that didn't belong to him. Suppose it belonged to Scrooge. What do you think Bob should do with it? Keep it or return it to the rightful owner?"

Mr Read was sitting down on his desk, typing something on his keyboard. His head was facing the monitor. At that moment, he suddenly stopped. He then closed his teacher planner, put the lid back on his red pen, put the whiteboard markers in their place, tidied the handouts and worksheets that were left over from the lesson and gave me a peculiar stare for about five seconds. It was as if he was saying: *Why on earth would you ask me that?*

Except he didn't say that. He scratched his head and continued casually. "Well... I think Bob Cratchit is a decent, sensible man who would always do the right thing. I don't think he would hold on to money that wasn't his, however tempting it was. Yes, I mean... he would definitely return the money and if he was scared of how Scrooge would react, he'd probably find a creative way to return it without letting Scrooge know that it was he who found the money in the first place. Maybe he'd put it somewhere it could be found easily by Scrooge. That's what Bob would do and that's what we should always do when faced with difficult decisions. We should always do the right thing."

That was it! My prayers were answered again alhamdulillah! I could easily sort out this problem and easily rid myself of this huge burden. I felt a huge sense of relief. It was an easy solution that had already occurred to me, but I didn't think of it as an option because I couldn't think straight. You see, we often do that when we are overwhelmed with problems. Often the answer is staring us right in the face. We just can't see it because we are so preoccupied with worry.

Dad was right. It is good to talk. Even though I didn't disclose everything to Mr Read, he probably had some idea. Sometimes, if possible, we just need to open up to someone, providing they can help. Just to explain our problems to a new set of ears, a new mind, so they can see through our cloudy judgement and offer some possible solutions.

I took a deep breath and left Mr Read's class feeling lighter. I felt a bit stupid for not realising how simple the solution was in the first place, but hey, at least now I knew what to do. The problem now was: how was I going to do it? I needed a plan, and fast.

* * *

On the way home from school, I stopped to pick up some bread and milk from Mr Cooper's shop. Riya was there picking up some groceries. I saw her looking at the Community Fridge and walked past her, pretending I didn't see her. I didn't want her to notice that I saw her looking at it. I headed straight for the seeded bread section and I saw from the corner of my eye that she noticed me. We already collected the items we needed from the Community Fridge earlier on in the week so I went straight for the cash desk.

"Hey, Aristotle," she called out in her soft voice. I shuddered, feeling my heart melt like caramel ice-cream.

"Riya! You're not following me, are you?" I joked. Why did I just say that? I asked myself, mentally kicking myself. How stupid of me! I hoped she didn't think I was trying to flirt with her. I was desperately trying not to.

"No, I'm not," she insisted, trying not to blush, except it didn't work. Her pale skin, which had a hint of olive, didn't turn bright red as she blushed. Instead her cheeks turned slightly dark, giving off a light purple hue. I had clearly embarrassed her.

"Sorry. I didn't mean to... I was just joking." I felt really guilty.

"It's okay," she replied, pretending that I didn't just make her blush. "Seeded bread, eh? Good choice. My dad loves that stuff."

"Yeah, I like it too. Makes a change from the usual brown or white." I realised how awkward I had made the whole conversation. "So, you good?" I asked.

"Yeah, same old," she replied, staring mindlessly at the cereal boxes to her right. It suddenly occurred to me that she was probably waiting for me to leave so that she could pick something from the Community Fridge. I so wanted to tell her everything, to get it off my chest. But the words were trapped in my throat. I looked into her eyes for a few seconds. If only she'd asked, I would have just burst out with everything that was on my mind. Instead, we said goodbye and took our separate ways.

Chapter 16

Mission Possible

Several days had now passed in this state of utter confusion. I was torn between dipping my hand into that bag to pay off those nasty bills and ease the burden on my family, and doing the right thing and getting rid of it. Whenever I saw Mum glance at the dreaded letter and rub her forehead and sigh, or whenever she apologised for not being able to get the ingredients for a nice dinner, the urge became overpowering. It was crazy to think that I had the power to end all of our problems, simply by placing my hand into that black bag. To say it was tempting would be an understatement. My mind forged endless possibilities of all the things that could happen as a result of my actions—or lack of.

Today, however, was a new day and for the first time in a long time I could see things clearly. Even though I was only halfway there, I felt a sense of relief. I'm almost there! Almost, I told myself. I had it all planned out in my head in intricate detail. I was going to do something that I should have done a long time ago: dump that cursed bag where I found it!

I left home slightly early that day. It was an unusually humid morning. It had rained the previous night and there was a strong, unpleasant stench of damp in the air. I glanced back to see the usual row of tower blocks looming over me. This time, though, the windows of people's flats turned into hundreds of menacing eyes. I looked up at them defiantly. No turning back now. Escaping their long, hard stares, I hurried along with the bag hidden under my jacket, tightly clutching it with my elbow and squeezing it towards my left rib cage. The trees were now within my sight and as I got ever closer, my heart began to race. I'm doing the right thing, I kept repeating to myself, something that I should have done a long time ago. In fact, what I should have done was not pick it up in the first place. So much regret, but still, at least I was trying to put it right now.

The tree was now a few steps away. The nerves kicked in. Adrenaline coursed through my body, making it stiff. I fought hard to keep moving, but my legs didn't want to obey. The stench of the rainfall wasn't helping me to slow my breathing down. Any moment, any moment now, I was going to pass out. I was so sure. But I hung on. I took a deep breath and let the bag slip out of my fingers at the exact spot in which I found it and continued along the leafy path way.

Finally! Finally, I was free! I realised how warm and flushed I felt, and my breathing still hadn't returned to normal, but I couldn't slow down. I made sure I was safely out of the vicinity before I came to a halt, panting. I looked back towards the row of menacing eyes peeping through the trees, taunting me, trying to tell me something. I didn't want to listen. It was over, I thought to myself. I wasn't scared anymore. My heart was waiting for relief, ready to enjoy its freedom, but for some reason, it wasn't coming. I no longer had that cursed black bag in my possession, but its burden hadn't lifted.

I tried to leave those feelings behind me as I walked to school ready to plough on through the day, but it was no use. I was on edge. I went from lesson to lesson feeling like an empty shell. I thought dropping that bag would make me feel happy and light, but for some reason it didn't. Instead, feelings of dread filled up my heart and mind like an unwanted spirit. It's over, I kept reassuring myself. Maybe a part of me wanted something terrible to happen so I could be punished for being so stupid in the first place.

To calm myself down, I decided to pray zuhr in the drama studio. By the time I completed my prayer, I started to feel slightly normal again. On the way home, I tried to focus on the here and now. I noticed everything in order to block out my worries: the grey clouds, the declining sunlight, the rustling of leaves as the wind blew mildly, the noisy mothers with their pushchairs as they hurried along with their small children. Everything is going to be alright, I thought, and for a moment, I truly believed it.

* * *

I slammed the door behind me, dropping my bag on the floor.

"Mum, I'm home," I called. My stomach gave a loud groan. "Have you cooked anything or shall I make something for dinner? I'm starving." I slumped down on the sofa, putting my feet up. What a day. I closed my eyes, trying to drift off.

My eyes sprang open again when I heard muffled shouts and heavy footsteps pounding down the hallway outside. I shot up, startled. Someone must have been getting evicted again.

But the sound crept closer and closer. A pause. Suddenly, a storm of fists began pounding on our front door, making the ground beneath us shake.

"Open the door!" yelled an angry voice. "NOW!"

I froze. My eyes flitted around, quickly trying to figure out what was going on. Who were they? And who were they after? Me? No. It wasn't possible.

"Nadim?" The small, fragile figure of my mum emerged behind me, her face contorted with worry.

"I said NOW!"

The walls of the flat were trembling with the sheer force of their blows, the door threatening to break. Without thinking, I ran to swing it open. Huge, dark figures pushed past me, with a menacing, barking dog. It tried to charge at me aggressively, but one of the men held on tightly to the leash.

"DON'T MOVE!" he boomed. "Put your hands behind your back!"

I did exactly as he asked. I tried to remain calm, but my heart was racing like it was going to rip out of my chest. Mum's deafening screams pierced the air. Musa was stood in the doorway, his mouth wide open, his forehead creased in a deep frown. He must have rushed over, having heard the commotion. The room was spinning. The thin, worn-out carpet beneath me began to feel thick and soft. I looked left and right. I had nowhere to go. Musa's face and the voices of the officers began to blur. I blinked several times to try and keep my eyes open, but it was no use—I was falling, falling into dismal darkness, with no end. I felt the hard floor press against my stomach, the harsh carpet brush against my face. Cold cuffs clasped around my wrists as the dog loomed over me, heavy and slobbering, drenching me in its saliva. I didn't realise I was crying until I tasted the saltiness of a tear on the tip of my tongue. The whirr of the police sirens in the distance was coming closer and closer. The last thing I saw was Mum with her right hand on her chest, panting heavily as she clung on to the kitchen door frame. Then everything went completely blank.

Chapter 17

Cell 6

When my eyes opened, I found myself lying on a hospital bed. Mum was there with the twins and there were two police officers, one inside the room and the other sat down just outside of the room. I saw Musa through the glass window of the door.

Dr Simmons told me that I had passed out and the police officers called an ambulance. The police officer informed me that as soon as I was fit and ready I would be formally arrested on suspicion of 'perverting the course of justice'. I didn't even know what that meant and I was still trying to get to grips with the fact that I had somehow wound up on a hospital bed.

About an hour later, I was discharged from the hospital and taken to the police station. Mum couldn't come with me as she had the twins with her, but she told me that she would come to the station after leaving them with Musa's mum. I saw Musa asking one of the officers if he could come in, but the arresting officer didn't allow him to enter the room and speak to me.

"I'm afraid he's not allowed to speak to anyone now, sir," insisted the officer in his formal, robotic voice. "He'll be placed under arrest and we'll take him to the police station shortly."

When I got there, they checked me in and placed me in Cell 6 until they were ready to interview me. I'll never forget the inside of that cell. It was very small, and being claustrophobic certainly didn't help. It was a square-shaped room with four walls and what looked like a bed and mattress against one wall. There were no sheets, just a plastic blue mattress and a matching pillow. They had taken away my clothes to send them to the forensics team to analyse so I was given white overalls to wear, the kind you might see builders or road sweepers wear. I felt humiliated.

The walls in the cell were particularly harsh. They reminded me of the lifeless walls of the tower blocks. They were covered from top to bottom with very revolting looking, light green coloured tiles. It felt like I'd been left in a big public toilet. The floors were muddy and dirty. On my left was a small toilet basin, but no sink or toilet paper. I wasn't planning on using it—just the look of it was horrible. It was metal and had visible traces of poo and urine stains around the bottom. It looked like it hadn't been cleaned for weeks, just like the lifts in our tower block. My only source of natural light was a small window right at the top of the cell, which was impossible for me to reach. Even that was covered with four metal bars on the inside. As I sat there on what was supposed to be a bed, every minute seemed to pass like an hour. There was no clock inside the cell so I banged my fist against the door to call for attention several times. All I asked for was the time. I would be sure that half an hour had passed, and then my heart would sink when I found out it had only been ten minutes. They stopped responding by the fourth time. They were probably keeping an eye on me from the camera in the corner of the cell.

They gave me a copy of the Qur'an to read, which I did, for some reason with a renewed sense of interest. The stories of the Prophets Yusuf and Yunus (may God's peace be upon them) seemed more relevant to me than ever. I read about the great tribulations Prophet Yusuf went through, from being thrown down a well by his own brothers, facing the temptations of a woman and then being wrongfully thrown into prison. Despite Allah blessing him with many of His bounties, Prophet Yusuf was also heavily tested and he got through it by being patient and calling upon Allah in du'a. Yes, I hadn't been thrown into a well, but I suppose I had been trying to resist the temptations of a girl. And as for being wrongfully imprisoned, that struck a chord with me the most. I was not a criminal, I had never committed a crime, yet I was being treated like one because I made one stupid mistake.

The story of Prophet Yunus reminded me that even in the deepest, darkest ocean, inside the belly of a whale, Allah the Almighty can hear you and respond to your du'as. I sang the famous Prophet Yunus *nasheed* in my head (the one Mum always sang when she felt a bit down). I knew my situation wasn't as extreme as that of the Prophet Yunus, but here I was in a cell by myself, with no family, no friends and no connection to the outside world. I used that lonely, isolated place to prostrate to Allah and raise my hands in du'a. I read the stories, recited, prayed and make dhikr, and felt peace and calm return to me.

After what felt like an eternity, they finally let me out to talk to the duty solicitor.

"Right, Mr Nadim Asad. The police have informed me what the allegations are and I have been asked to represent you in a police interview," he said. "My name is Mark Hammond. Pleased to meet you," he continued, holding out his hand.

"Officer, there's been a terrible mistake. I'm not a criminal, honest," I pleaded whilst shaking his hand vigorously.

"I'm not an officer," he interrupted. "I'm a solicitor and I will be advising you and representing you. I am here to advise you what is best for your current predicament."

Somehow his words soothed me and I listened attentively.

"I must advise you to be as honest as possible with the police. They will ask you a series of questions in the interview. Please answer them as best you can," he advised. "Since you have no previous convictions, I should think they'll release you on bail today as long as they can see that you are cooperating."

That's exactly what I did. I told them everything from the beginning to the end and how I regretted ever picking up that bag. The interview lasted approximately twenty-five minutes and I was released on bail with the condition that I returned to the police station two weeks later once they finished their investigations. At that point they would tell me if they were going to formally charge me with anything.

At the end of the interview, they brought me out through the front entrance. "I'll be in touch, Nadim." Mark flung on his coat, put a bundle of papers into his briefcase and walked out of the station using the glass doors.

involved in something linked to the street boys. All of this because of one tiny wrong action. It seemed to me that wrong things were the easiest to carry out, but the most difficult to put right again.

Chapter 18

Life on Bail

The next fortnight was one of the most difficult times of my entire life. I couldn't help but feel like a criminal because I was still 'under investigation'. Everything in my life suffered: my friendships, my family life, my studies, my sleep and even my physical health, not to mention my mental well-being.

I saw much less of my friends because I didn't want to be around anyone. All I wanted was to be alone. Even when I was with them, my mind was so preoccupied with other things that I could barely keep up with the conversation or laugh at anybody's jokes. I stopped going to the mosque and I stopped the jogging, gym and kick-boxing sessions with Musa. What was the point? He called several times and knocked at my front door, but I didn't answer or return his calls. I told Mum to tell him that I didn't want to see anyone. I just wanted to be left alone.

I spent most of my time in my bedroom. I couldn't face Mum. She must have felt so ashamed finding me in a hospital bed surrounded by police officers and then having to pick me up from the police station. We both avoided the subject if it came up, but I knew she was in close contact with Mark, my solicitor, in case he had any important updates.

My sleep... oh Allah, I'd have done anything for a good night's sleep. I tried everything: I did some light exercises in the evening to try and tire myself out, I drank a cup of warm milk before sleeping, I even tried chamomile tea (I read somewhere that it was a natural remedy for insomnia), but nothing worked... nothing. I wanted to purchase Nytol from the chemist, but they wouldn't sell it to me, and I wouldn't have been able to afford it anyway. My nights consisted of tossing and turning in bed and fighting with my mind, trying to make it switch off, but it refused. I felt like I'd been pushed right to the edge, but I knew I couldn't give up. I remembered Mum's words on the day she picked me up from the police station, about how she couldn't bear to lose me. *Not again and not with you.* I had to keep moving forward. I wasn't going to let life swallow me up. Losing one or two battles during the day was a possibility, but giving up on life never was!

I went to school like a zombie because of the lack of sleep. Because I couldn't concentrate in class my grades at the next assessment point dropped, in some subjects by almost two grades. I made no progress in that half-term, but the school understood because they knew what happened and the stress that I was under. My Head of Year, Ms Thomas, always checked up on me when she could. But to be honest, I felt like no one could help. I just needed to go back to the police station and face whatever they were going to do to me. And for that, I had to wait patiently.

Halfway through the first week, Ms Thomas called me into her office for a chat, despite always looking like she was rushed off her feet. School was like that. They spent so much time on the troublesome kids that good students like me often just hovered through each term, unless, of course, we did something wrong or stepped out of line.

"Nadim, I'm concerned about you," she said. "I know about all the trouble you've faced over the last week or so, but I want you to know that I'm always here if you need anything, okay?"

"Thanks, Miss," I replied mechanically.

"You know why I've called you into my office, right?" she asked, searching through a pile of papers until she reached my half-term grades card. A copy had already been sent home so I knew how bad it was.

"I know how bad it looks, Miss... but I just can't focus with all this stuff hanging over my head. I feel like I'm going mad!"

"Nadim, sometimes life is just like that unfortunately. You don't get one problem but several, all at the same time." Her face creased into a frown as her eyes scanned my report card from top to bottom.

"I know how bad it is, Miss," I said quickly, before she could comment.

"Despite the problems we all face, Nadim, you have to stay focused. You're in Year 11 now and only a few months away from your final exams. You can't afford to drop this much."

"I can climb back up, Miss, you know I can." I tried to sound convincing.

"You can, yes, but the question is, will you? Despite whatever is going on, Nadim, I want you to focus, prioritise and get on with it. When you're in school try to block out everything that's happening outside and focus on your work. When you've completed all of your exams, you'll have the longest holiday ever. Do what you want then, but for now I want you to focus and concentrate. One hundred and ten percent! You understand?"

"Yes, Miss. I understand." I knew she was right. I just thought it was easier said than done.

"Look, you're a good student—one of the few that will do well and make the school proud. You've always been a hard worker. Don't let that slip now no matter what else is going on in your life. If you need any help, support or even counselling, just come and see me and I'll do whatever I can."

"Counselling?" I frowned. "I'm not a loony, Miss."

"I never said you were, but we all need someone to talk to sometimes, someone that can maybe make you see things in a different light and help you find some solutions, or at least help you find ways to cope."

"Thanks but I'm alright, Miss."

I left Ms Thomas' office thinking about what she said. Yes, I did need to focus and prioritise and maybe, just maybe, I might benefit from some counselling. But I didn't want to. What if people at school found out I was speaking to a counsellor? They'd all have a right laugh. Razor and his cronies would have a field day!

* * *

I spent so much time alone in my room that I'd even stopped eating or making dinner for everyone else. Mum started cooking again and a couple of times she made really delicious food like fish and chips or oven-baked pizzas. But nothing appealed to me. I usually ate half of what Mum served on the plate just to keep her happy and often at night, when the anxiety got really bad, I threw up most of what I ate. I needed to get a grip on things. I couldn't go on like this! But I knew I had to until the fortnight passed.

One night, when I was struggling to sleep, I had the urge to get up and leave. I needed to get out of the flat and do something, although I didn't know what. Still wearing my pyjamas, I put on my trainers and tracksuit top and tread across the living room, trying really hard not to make so much as a squeak. Once I heard the click of the door close behind me, I fled down the staircase (whilst trying not to inhale the repugnant smell of urine) and flew out of our main communal entrance.

I stopped and stood there for a while just staring at the stillness of the night. It must have been about 2am. I saw the lights turned off in most of the flats in our block and the surrounding blocks, but the street lights were dimly lit. The road leading out of our estate was also very quiet, with a car passing every couple of minutes. I blinked a few times to adjust my vision and shake off the tiny amount of tiredness that I felt, even though my mind was working faster than a speeding train. I took a deep breath, inhaling the fresh air. In the distance, I spotted the street boys doing what they usually did at this time. The night provided a perfect cover for their sinister activities. They saw me standing outside my building but paid no attention to me.

I put on my hood, zipped up my jumper and ran. I was by myself—no Musa supporting me this time. I just ran. I didn't know where I was running to, but I knew I just wanted to run. At first I was running quickly and then slowed down to bring myself to a steady jogging pace. I ran down Regent's Canal westwards into unknown territory. I passed by the lavish new build properties that boasted 'waterside views' and past a long line of canal boats. The new build development had scaffolding all around it and was boarded up around the bottom part, but was still covered in bright advertising posters that were lit up by spotlights. The posters had amazing, beautiful flats plastered all over and boasted of 'communal swimming pools, gyms and private cinemas'. These flats clearly weren't for the local community. No one I knew could afford them. They were probably designed to attract posh, rich city workers. The canal boats sat still on the water with their doors locked, ropes attaching them to the concrete pathway, making only slight movements as the wind blew mildly.

I ran for a long time. I don't know how many miles I ran and I don't know how long I ran for. Before I knew it, I ended up in Camden Lock, which was miles from where I lived. I was a little exhausted, but energetic at the same time. Maybe this was why they gave people bail, I thought, to make you suffer and break you down mentally and physically. If that was the aim, then it certainly worked on me. I focused my mind on the scenery to block out the aggressive, brutal and insidious thoughts that tried to invade my mind. I started to run back in the direction of our estate but I didn't stop when I passed home. I just ran and ran. Deep down I knew where I needed to go.

I walked up to the front gate. I gave it a little push and it creaked open. The front gates were well-lit with security cameras surrounding the entrances. I walked in, passed the car park and crossed over a small bridge. It looked much more full than when I last visited. People say graveyards are scary and haunted places, but I never felt scared here. Instead, I felt peace and tranquillity. I passed by many graves of men, women, children and even still-born infants before I finally reached Dad's spot.

As I reached the headstone, a colossal amount of sadness overcame me. I stood looking down at his place of rest. I felt so helpless. All the feelings and emotions I felt when he first died started to rise up in my chest, amplified by the emotions I was going through because of this whole ordeal.

I couldn't walk anymore. I sat exactly where six feet underneath his face must have been. I sat there, paralysed by sadness. Cold sweat ran down my face. I tried to warm my hands by rubbing them against my legs, but it was no use. The night time chill combined with the emptiness I felt inside only made my sadness grow. The mud around the graveyard was a reminder that my Dad was under all of this and no longer with me. A physical barrier between us, forever.

The overwhelming emotions were too much. I wasn't able to contain myself. The tears burst out like water from an irreparable burst water pipe, spilling down my face, leaving long string-like traces down my cheeks. I felt the muscles of my chin tremble, shaking as if electricity was passing through. I heard myself letting out giant sobs, louder than I ever heard Mum do, even when she left Nabil at the end of the visits. I cried and I cried, so loudly that the sound of my own sobbing was beginning to ring in my ears. I saw that the graveyard was empty so I made no effort to control or compose myself. I cried like an abandoned baby, desolate and hysterical, but I couldn't help myself. The rain started to fall in a constant drizzle, blending with my tears and blurring my vision.

Still sobbing, I began to shout.

"Why did you have to die?" I shouted. "Why? Mum needs you! The twins need you! Nabil needs you and I need you too! I need you, Dad! Why did you have to suddenly leave us? You didn't even give us time to grow up and prepare. You just left. I can't be you. I don't know how to be you. I can't fill your shoes. They're too big."

I knew he couldn't hear me but I couldn't stop. I needed to speak to him, tell him everything I'd been bottling up since he died.

The anguish made my heart feel like it was about to explode. The feeling of deep distress caused by loss, disappointment and all of the misfortunes I faced throughout my short life seemed to weigh heavily upon my heart.

I felt the numbness of my face in the cold. I was on my knees but I was stumbling, losing my balance. My eyes were shutting. I closed them for a second. My head was light and spinning like I was inside a dark washing machine, slowly spinning. I tried to open my eyes again, but I couldn't. All of a sudden I felt myself stumble forward. I went down like a sack of rice and landed on my face. I lay there in the dirt, still as a corpse, but with my head spinning in the dismal blackness of my unconscious mind. Everything fell silent.

I saw Dad again for the first time since we lost him. He looked well, dressed in his favourite pin-stripe, dark navy, custom-made three-piece suit that Mum bought for him for their tenth anniversary. His jet black hair was neatly pushed back, exposing his forehead. His beard was trimmed neatly like it used to be when he was alive. His glowing skin looked warm and healthy. He was trying to speak, trying to say something to me, but I couldn't work out what. I walked towards him.

"Nadim! Be strong, be firm, be resolute and have an unbreakable iron will," he said softly. "Be at peace within yourself, Nadim. Let your heart and mind be at peace, my son. Push your anger aside, take a deep breath and squeeze all the hurt and pain out of your heart. You have a loving family, a sound mind, a firm heart and working limbs. Be thankful to Allah," he said, embracing me as I struggled to contain my sobs. "These things should always renew your strength to carry on. As long as you always try your best, to be the best you can be, who can defeat you? Trust in Allah, take action, keep going and all will be well... my son."

* * *

I woke up to the noise of a tractor that was digging and preparing a grave a few rows away from me. What was going on? Where was I? I looked at my watch. It was 9am. I was late for school and here I was, lying in a graveyard and covered in mud. Mum must be worried sick, I thought to myself. Hopefully she didn't realise that I left home at night time. And what about the twins? I gasped.

My clothes stuck to my body because of the dried up sweat from the previous night. My entire body was stiff with aches and pains. I clambered myself up and decided I was going to get home, have a shower, get changed and get myself to school.

It was a fairly chilly morning. It was bright, but not warm at all. I heard the sound of birds flying above me muffled by the chatter of young children coming from somewhere on our block. I walked down the stairs and past the cleaner. He passed his wet mop over the stairs and the yellow ceramic tiles that covered the bottom half of the staircase walls. It didn't make much difference—they still looked hideous. I shuddered, remembering those grisly green coloured tiles from Cell 6 at the police station. Passing by the graffiti-covered walls, I bumped into Musa at the bottom of the staircase.

"Salaam!" he said, giving me a wide smile.

"Wa-alaykum salaam," I replied. I realised how long it had been since we last spoke and felt embarrassed thinking about all his calls that I'd failed to return.

"Shattered today. I should have finished my shift two hours ago," he yawned, rubbing his eyes. "But I had to cover for another colleague so I did part of his round too. Alhamdulillah, it's all good. Bit of overtime always helps at the end of the month!"

"Yeah, deffo."

There was an awkward pause.

"Anyway, how you doing, bro? Haven't seen you in a while. You haven't been coming to the mosque and we haven't jogged together for ages or done any training." He took off his empty postman bag and rested it on the floor.

"Things have been really hard lately," I explained.

"Yeah I know, I saw you that time when the police officers, y'know... and then I was at the hospital," he said. "I tried calling you, bro, and I came asking for you, but after a while I thought you just needed some space so I left you alone."

"I know. I'm really sorry, Musa. I didn't mean to... I mean, I should have returned your calls."

"Nah, it's okay! It's fine, seriously," he insisted. "It's good to see you, man. How you holding up?"

"Not great, to be honest. I feel like I've let everyone down... I shouldn't have picked up that stupid bag in the first place... had enough trouble to deal with even before the bag... why was I so stupid? I... I should have just... I don't know, man, I was just desperate... confused... curious, but I should have known better, I should have.... I didn't pick it up thinking it would make me accidentally rich, I didn't even know what was inside it. I shouldn't have done it... I..."

"Hey, take it easy! Don't be so hard on yourself, man," he interrupted. "We all make mistakes." He placed his right hand on my shoulder.

"It's a pretty big mistake. You know what kind of person that bag belongs to, don't you?"

"Yeah, but they don't know who picked up their bag, and no one else saw you get arrested. I'm quite sure I was the only person around to see all that commotion."

"They'll probably be after me when they find out and I'll probably go to jail when I return to the station after bail."

"Don't be stupid," he said, trying to keep his voice down. "What did the police say and what did you say to them?"

"I told them the truth: that it didn't belong to me and that I picked it up and then realised that I shouldn't have and then tried to put it back where I found it."

"Yeah and what did they say to that?"

"They just said I should return after two weeks after they've done some more investigations."

"Yeah, that's good. If they had something on you, trust me, they would have charged you already. You've been honest with them and you haven't done anything wrong. You just made a silly mistake, which you tried to put right. And about those street rats, don't worry. They don't know and they won't find out... just don't speak to anyone else about this."

"Okay," I replied, letting out a sigh of distress.

"Trust me, it will all be good inshallah. Make du'a to Allah, be strong and don't let things weigh you down. It's gonna be fine. You'll return to the police station at the end of your bail period and they'll probably thank you for being so honest with them, alright?"

"Okay," I mumbled. "I've got to run now. I'm late already."

"I hope to see you at the mosque tonight inshallah. Don't worry about the training, we'll come back to that when you're ready."

"Okay. Thanks, bro. I really appreciate it." I was still covered in mud and even more late for school, but I felt a little lighter and more optimistic having spoken to Musa.

* * *

By the time I got to school, it was break time. I signed in late and headed for the Humanities corridor waiting for the pips to sound. I had double History next. With my backpack firmly attached, I ran straight into Razor and his three stooges. Great.

"Watch yourself you..." he muttered under his breath before he turned around. "Oi! Come back here!" he yelled. I shouldn't have, but I stopped and turned around, thinking if I didn't, they would hunt me down afterwards anyway. The four of them walked towards me, fists clenched, with the look of death on all of their faces. Razor came right up to my face, his cheeks flaring up as he ground his teeth.

"What do you want?" I asked, trying not to sound rude.

"You don't just bump into mans like me, y'understand?" I sensed the anger brewing in his voice. He looked at me, his eyes bloodshot red and his face screwed up like a scrunched up paper bag.

"Look, I was in a hurry. I didn't see you guys. I'm sorry," I said sincerely.

"Nah, you don't get away with it that easily!" His goons surrounded me. "Empty out your pockets you dirty little tramp. Let's see what you have for us! Then maybe I'll let it slide."

I didn't want to empty out my pockets. All I had with me was my phone and the open bottle of water I was holding in my hand. I wasn't going to let them take my phone. With my heart pounding and the blood hot in my veins, I was on the brink of losing my patience. I tried to restrain my anger because I didn't want to fight. Besides, I was outnumbered four to one.

"Sure," I said, reaching into my pockets with my left hand. For a few brief seconds I thought about what I could do to get myself out of the situation until I looked at the bottle of cold water in my hand, still almost full. I threw it on Razor's face, pushing past him as the cold water temporarily blinded him and then made a run for it. I ran past the Humanities corridor, scraping my arm on the wall displays as I squeezed through a couple of girls who were walking towards me.

I turned around to look back. "Sort him out, boys!" yelled Razor, wiping his face with his forearm. "Don't let him get away!"

I turned right into the wide corridor where the Music classes were. I looked into every classroom—they were empty. I headed straight for the Main Hall and slammed on the big wide doors, which were usually left open, but not this time. They were closed and could only be opened from the inside. I pulled at the doors frantically, but nothing happened. There was no escape. Razor and his gang turned the same corner. They saw me trapped. A wide grin appeared on his face.

"Easy, boys," he laughed. "Where you gonna run now?" They walked straight towards me slowly in a horizontal line, their hands stretched out so I couldn't get past them again.

It happened so quickly. I was knocked backwards by the power of Razor's push and fell onto the glass doors of the Main Hall. Then I felt a barrage of angry fists pound me in every part of my body. It was all a blur. I didn't know where or who they were exactly coming from. I tried to keep my guard up and move around to try and protect my face the way Musa showed me. But it was no use. I felt punches to the back of my head, ears and temples. The pain shot through my body like jolts of electricity. Just then, in the middle of what felt like a thunderstorm, I saw Razor's face, right there in front of me. I stood up, guarding my face with my left hand. I pulled back my clenched right fist and swung it around, pushing my entire body forward with all my weight behind me. It connected with his jaw bone and made an exploding sound like a small clap of thunder. I couldn't help myself. The adrenaline, the fear—it was like nothing I had experienced before. I followed it with a blow to his right rib, several punches to his chest, stomach, and face and then a knee to his groin. I ended my rage with a final uppercut to his chin. He fell to the floor backwards like a tall tree being cut at the base by a chainsaw. For a second, everything stopped. They all looked at me in utter bewilderment and shock.

"What's going on down there?" a loud voice boomed down the corridor.

Razor's gang of three scattered like frightened mice. I was left standing there, my fists throbbing and Razor lying there at my feet. He was unconscious. When the adrenaline disappeared, the guilt started churning in my stomach as I looked down to see Razor lying on his back. I couldn't feel the bloodied cuts on my face or the swollen bruises on the back of my head, arms and legs. All I felt was a sense of horror flood through me, realising what I'd just done.

Chapter 19

It Wasn't Me!

I perched nervously on the chair outside the Head of Year's office. Ms Thomas had to do a follow-up regarding the incident and then tidy up all the paperwork first before deciding what to do with me. School was always like this when incidents happened—so much paperwork and 'investigation' even though the end result was the same. I held my head in my hands, shaking my head in disbelief. I knew I was looking at an exclusion. I couldn't believe I was in this situation, so close to my final exams! This was definitely not how I imagined spending the last of my school days. I had to make sure I could avoid it. I wrote out my statement for Ms Thomas, being as open and honest as I could. I told her exactly what happened.

"Right. In you get then." I could hear the disappointment in her sharp voice before I even looked up. She closed the door behind her even though the room was stuffy due to the poor ventilation system. That only meant one thing: she was going to yell at me.

"What on earth is going on?" she screamed. "You, Nadim, are one of those very few students in Year 11 that I've been pinning my hopes on. It's students like YOU who I hope will do well and do us proud and now you've gone and done something as thoughtless as this?"

"Miss, didn't you read my—?"

"Yes, I've read your statement." I tried to interject but only a feeble sound escaped my lips before she yelled, "Stop talking! There's absolutely no justification for what you did, Nadim. You knocked him unconscious for crying out loud! Yes, I know Rachid is a trouble maker, but why didn't you just tell a member of staff instead of launching into him?"

"Miss, I was trying to defend myself from four of them. Four against one! What did you expect me to do? Nobody was around! They could have seriously hurt me!"

She let out a long sigh. "You know what I'm going to have to do, don't you? You know the school policy."

My heart sank. "Yes. Yes, I know the school policy, Miss."

"Look, you're a good student and this is really out of character for you, which is why I'm going to give you a fixed term exclusion for five days. You are to leave the premises immediately and not come anywhere near the school building for that time period. When you return, I need your mum here to sign a contract in your Return to School meeting with the Head and myself. I'll call home and speak to your mum a bit later. For now, I'm going to deal with Rachid and his gang."

That was it. To top it all off, I knew Razor had links with the street boys who roamed around outside our flat so I didn't feel safe walking home from school. I called Musa to come and pick me up.

I stepped outside as soon as he arrived. It was mid-afternoon and the daylight was slowly declining. The clouds gathered and swelled. It looked like it was going to rain, but the sky somehow managed to hold back its tears. I was disappointed with myself. Disappointed that I lost control. I didn't feel like myself. Acting out violently... that wasn't me at all. The frightening thing was that a part of me didn't even regret hitting Razor. I shuddered. These changes were beginning to scare me. I wished I hadn't hit him so hard, I wished I hadn't hit him at all. I caught sight of him sitting outside the Head of Year's office as I left. His face was red, angry and bulging with cuts and sores. It wasn't a pretty sight. Deep down, I felt sorry for him. Maybe there were reasons why he acted the way he did, but I'd never know. Maybe it didn't even matter. In the end, it's our actions that define us.

* * *

It was a short drive home. Musa and I didn't speak during the whole journey. I stared out of the window, listening to the recitation of the Qur'an playing in his car. As we approached our tower block, he parked up and turned the engine off. He turned his body towards me.

"You wanna talk about what happened?" he asked in his usual mild-mannered tone, his eyebrows slightly raised.

I took in a deep breath. "It wasn't my fault, it was that Razor. He just goes around with his mates picking on everyone, thinking he owns the school. But... I shouldn't have reacted like that. I hurt him pretty bad. Knocked him out cold. I'm not proud of myself," I added quickly.

"I told you," said Musa quietly, "when I first started training you that this stuff is only to make you feel more confident, help you de-stress and get your fitness levels up. Yes, I know, I did say you can use it for self-defence, but only when really necessary, bro. Not in school. Not in a silly fight. You said he was out cold, man. You could have seriously hurt the guy!"

I gulped. "I know. I really let you down, Musa. I'm sorry. It's just that he really wound me up and had me up against one corner. The four of them, Razor and his three goons, were going at me like there was no tomorrow. It felt like they were never going to stop. I just felt this rage boil up in my blood and take over my whole body. I reacted before I even realised what I was doing. What would you have done?"

"I would have blocked them, pushed them aside and ran to find a teacher. That would have been the right thing to do. I wouldn't have engaged cos I know how much I can hurt someone. This body of yours is an *amaana*, a trust from Allah, a gift. And now you have extra skills and abilities. You should never use the gifts and abilities that Allah has blessed you with to do evil. You understand?"

I hung my head in shame. "Yeah, I do. I'm sorry."

"It's more beloved to Allah if you can restrain yourself in a moment of anger because that's really hard. Not everyone can hold themselves back when they're angry, but that's why it's a test. You have to always try to do the right thing despite anything that is going on in your life or around you. Anyway, I don't wanna lecture you anymore. Go home and get some rest. It's your big day soon. You need to focus on that."

Musa was right. I should have restrained myself. I shouldn't have acted out like that, no matter what Razor did to provoke me. I should have been the bigger man and walked away. I wouldn't make any more excuses for myself. Now that the adrenaline had worn off, the guilt hit me. I felt guilty about taking momentary pleasure from hitting Razor and guilty about how it would affect Mum when she found out. She already had a fragile heart with everything she'd been through and was still going through. I was the one holding it together, taking care of both Mum and the twins and now I'd just added another item to her list of worries. I had to change my ways and go back to being the responsible, mature young man that Mum and Nabil always praised. But I couldn't do that until I set right everything I'd done wrong. I needed to return to the police station and face whatever fate they decided for me. I needed to return to school after the exclusion and focus on acing my exams. I needed to take lessons from all the crazy things that seemed to be hitting me all in one go and come out the other end a renewed and improved person. I had to take the hits, the blows, the punches. I couldn't escape from them. Just like in the kick-boxing lessons I took with Musa, I had to learn how to defend myself from them and keep going. That's what I set out to do.

I stepped into our flat nervously. I saw Mum lying on the sofa, her eyes closed. Maybe she was asleep? I tread past her gently, trying to quietly head to my room.

"Ms Thomas called and spoke to me," said a voice behind me. I turned around. She was sitting up straight on the sofa, staring directly at me. Her expression was plain—no sign of disappointment, anger or frustration. Just a blank stare. Maybe it hasn't sunk in yet, I thought to myself, or maybe she'd been through so much that she was just numb to it all.

"I don't want to talk about this now, Nadim. I know you've been through a lot lately. Let's just focus on getting through Monday, okay?" Her tone was mild and casual. I nodded and left her to go to my room, dreading how she would react when she finally did want to talk about it, but luckily that time never came. She left me alone. I felt so grateful to her for her silent understanding, and for giving me the space I desperately needed.

Chapter 20

The Time Had Come

By the time the two weeks of my bail time were up, it felt like I'd been on a long marathon with huge obstacles in my path, obstacles that hit me in every part of my body to stop me from reaching the finish line. There were two more days left of my exclusion until I could return to school, but for now, I had to focus on returning to the police station to face whatever fate Allah had decided for me.

It was Monday morning and I was due to present myself at the police station by 11am. All the worry, stress and anxiety had been building up for the past two weeks for this moment. The agony of the wait was finally over, but the uncertainty of what lay ahead was terrifying. I told myself that I was honest with the police and that I would embrace any decision. In every problem, situation or difficulty in life, there are opportunities for growth, self-reflection and self-discovery. No matter what the outcome, I was hopeful that this scenario would end positively and would be an opportunity for me to grow.

As we walked up the stairs of the police station, my legs turned to jelly. I tried to compose myself. I didn't want Mum to see how scared I really was because she looked petrified herself. She kept on fidgeting with her fingers and biting her lips when I wasn't looking. When she did catch me looking, she would give me a smile and say, "Don't worry, son, it will all be okay inshallah."

We met Mark, my solicitor, at the entrance of the police station. He was dressed in a smart suit with a black tie. He looked like he was ready to go to a funeral. The thought made me feel nauseous.

"Okay, young man, let's get this over with," he smiled.

He looked serious but relaxed. I didn't understand how he could be so calm. But I guess this was his job and he'd probably done hundreds of bail appearances in his lifetime.

I uttered *bismillah* as we stepped inside. I looked around, noticing the dirty spotted blue liner on the floors, which reminded me of hospitals. The blue desk in front of us had a huge, thick glass which reached the ceiling like they had in banks and post offices with a few holes to speak through, but there was nobody behind the glass. There were no police officers to be seen. How is anyone supposed to report a crime if there are no officers at the front desk? I thought to myself. It looked eerily empty, like a scene from an apocalyptic movie where everyone had abandoned the city.

I gulped as my stomach began to churn. I felt my mouth drying up again. It felt like I was waiting to be executed. I didn't know what to expect. I looked at the water machine on my right, desperately wanting a cup of water, but the tank was empty and there were no plastic cups to be seen.

Finally, Mark stepped forward and used the telephone that was on the wall beside the front desk to tell them that we'd arrived. He put the phone down and waited for the investigating officer to take us through to an interview room. The wait was nerve-racking. I couldn't stop biting my nails and gritting my teeth. I didn't even realise I was doing it. I tried to slow down my breathing but that didn't work, since I was finding it hard to inhale.

After a few minutes, DCI Huntley came through and took us through the secure doors and into an empty room. There was nobody else there and there was no recording equipment either, which I thought was strange. I mean, if they had further questions for me, then surely they would want to record it again like they did the first time?

DCI Huntley sat us down. I sat at the table with Mark and Mum perched on a seat behind us.

"Mr Asad, we've concluded our investigations," she began in a clear voice. "My colleagues and I have looked at this extensively and we have listened to what you said at the interview. Firstly, we want to say thank you for being open and honest with us. Apart from the money, what you didn't spot was that hidden underneath a zipper at the bottom of that black bag were mobile phone chips, which provided us with crucial intelligence to make further arrests and put key members of the Masked Manz gang behind bars at last. It was members of the Masked Manz gang who burgled your home and other homes on your estate not long ago. That bag, young man, provided us with the final pieces of evidence that we needed to convict those criminals, who will be behind bars for a long time. This has only been possible because you put the bag back where you found it. You obviously had no idea, but we had the whole area under police surveillance after we arrested a gang member there that night. That was how we spotted you dropping a suspicious item on the day you got arrested, and we had to investigate further in case you were affiliated with the gang in any way. However, it quickly transpired that that wasn't the case." She smiled.

"Oh, and speaking of burglaries, you'll be delighted to know that we've also located the jewellery that was stolen from your home. We'll have that returned to you in due course after it gets released from the evidence room. The Masked Manz gang are part of a much bigger, wider network of organised criminals, but for now we're glad we've got some of them behind bars." I inhaled sharply. "But you certainly won't be. We have decided to drop the case against you—a 'No Further Action' in legal terms."

I just stared at her in disbelief. For a few seconds, that's all I did. I just looked at her mouth. Did those words just come out of that mouth? I didn't know how to process it. It wasn't what I was expecting at all.

Before I could look at Mum or Mark, the officer spoke again. "There is just one more thing... as a token of our appreciation, the Chief Inspector has decided to reward you for your honesty and for helping us tackle this crime. As you may know already, we launched an online campaign and offered a £5,000 reward for any information leading to the conviction of the Masked Manz gang and since you provided us with that final piece of the puzzle, we feel that the money should rightfully go to you. It's not a huge, astronomical amount," she continued, smiling, "it won't transform you into a rich man, but I'm sure you can enjoy it with your family."

My jaw dropped. I couldn't believe it! It was as if all of my prayers for all of these months had been answered all at once! Alhamdulillah!

Not only was I absolved of any criminal charges relating to holding that money, but I had actually been rewarded for my honesty! I can't describe the waves of happiness and shock that rippled through my body. I jumped up in joy, allowing the feelings to burst out.

Mum just looked at me as tears of joy rolled down her face. She didn't say anything. She just hugged me, holding me tightly to her chest.

Mark smiled. "Time to go home, then," he said, casual as ever. He then began to sign some papers that the officers handed to him. "Just formalities," he reassured us.

I walked home feeling like I was flying. My body was on the ground, but my heart and mind were free: free from the anxiety that had brought me to breaking point in the last two weeks, free from the fear of what might have happened to my family if anything happened to me, free from the guilt that had been weighing heavily on my heart and free from worrying about how we were going to pay off our next bill. It was all over.

* * *

I met up with Musa after the isha prayers. He was eager to find out what happened.

"So tell me what went down, man," he asked.

"What went down where?"

"Come on, man! Stop playin'! You know, at the station!"

I couldn't contain it any longer. "Alhamdulillah," I beamed, "no charges!"

"Mashallah, bro! *Allahu akbar!* That's great news!" He whooped, almost jumping up in the air. "Right, we gotta celebrate! There's a new dessert place opened up just behind the mosque. I say we hit that now—my treat!"

"Let's do it," I replied. "But it's my treat, okay?"

"If you insist, mate." He glanced at me sideways, giving me a peculiar look.

We arrived at the Snow Cake and took our seats on their loud orange leather seats. I ordered two scoops of honeycomb ice-cream with chai. Musa went for the Oreo milkshake and cake with custard.

"I always get the cake and custard," he said, unfolding his napkin and wiping his spoon clean with it. "It reminds of school dinners. The good old days," he laughed.

We sat there by the window, sipping our drinks and taking mouthfuls of our delicious desserts. I watched the worshippers as they left the mosque by the back entrance: some by themselves, some in couples, some with their friends and others holding hands with their young children. The sky was dark, clear and silent with not a single cloud in sight. The moon was clear and bright and reflected off the windows of the mosque. I felt a moment of calm wash over me. I looked at all of those people, who must all have had their own troubles, anxieties and worries. But they're getting on with it, I thought. That's what I needed to do now. Put the past behind me and look onwards and upwards.

I looked around Snow Cake, not wanting to stare, but admiring its decorations: the drooping lamp shades with soft lights, the white and brown floor tiles, the different flavoured ice-creams at the front counter, the three-dimensional black tiles behind it where glossy pictures of different desserts, shakes and mocktails were plastered. Just at that moment, Riya walked in. She didn't see us sitting on the far side. I looked at her closely, focusing on her fair, olive-tinted skin. She looked upwards at the glossy pictures with her light brown gazelle eyes and dark eyelashes. I watched her full lips move as she gave her order to the girl behind the counter. I remembered her voice, as smooth as velvet and sweet as honey. I wanted to get up and speak to her, but I knew I couldn't. The bliss and ecstasy I felt temporarily blinded me. I imagined going over there, talking to her, asking her what she'd like and then sitting down with her at the table, enjoying each other's company while we sipped our drinks and devoured our red velvet cakes with raspberry ripple ice-cream. *Astaghfirullah*, snap out of it, I told myself. I looked away, hoping Musa hadn't noticed.

"Do you know her?" he asked, with a mild frown.

"Just a girl from my year at school... well, primary school actually," I replied, trying hard to sound casual. "I don't really *know* her, know her. I mean, we sometimes speak when we bump into each other. But that's it."

"Careful there, bro," he joked, "don't be crossing any limits. I know what you teenagers are like."

"Don't be stupid," I snapped. "I'd never do anything like that. Besides, my Mum would kill me if she even thought I had a female friend let alone anything beyond that, so let's not go there!"

"Alright," he agreed, noticing that I was slightly annoyed. He changed the subject promptly. "Alhamdulillah, it worked out for you. You can't seem to take that smile off your face, mashallah. Anyone would think you're in one of those toothpaste adverts showing off your perfect white teeth," he joked. "It's good, though. I'm really happy for you. I told you, in the end everything will work out. You just need to have tawakkul in Allah and keep going. Allah never promised that this world was gonna be easy, but He promised that He will always be with you if you have patience. That's what we all need, bro. Patience and reliance upon Allah. If we can master that, we'll feel free from the prison of this dunya. This world is beneath your feet, so don't carry it on your shoulders!"

I nodded. I felt I finally understood the truth and wisdom in those words. I glanced at Riya from the corner of my eye. She picked up her scoop of ice cream and was leaving. She probably lived somewhere nearby. I sighed, trying to focus. Just one more thing I needed to sort in my life: my return back to school so I could ace those exams at the end of the year.

Chapter 21

The Return

Wednesday morning: the day of my return to school. I was ready for it. The storm was over. The only thing that now stood between me and returning to a normal life was this very serious interview with Ms Thomas and the Headteacher.

Mum and I arrived very early and sat on the green chairs just outside the Headteacher's office. We signed in at Reception. After a short wait, the pips sounded for the first lesson and I saw Ms Thomas and the Headteacher walking down the corridor, clutching various files and murmuring in hushed voices. They abruptly stopped when they saw us.

"Please come this way," said the Headteacher, as he led us into the small meeting room.

I saw Ms Thomas catch his eye, indicating that the meeting should commence. "Well," he began, clearing his throat. "I hope that this period of exclusion has allowed you time to reflect on the values that we hold dear in this school." His tone was very formal. I didn't want to argue back with him or defend myself despite all of the justifications and explanations I was dying to blurt out, so I just put my head down and nodded in agreement. I was genuinely remorseful. Turning to Mum, the Head continued. "Mrs Asad, we are aware that Nadim is a very bright boy and all of his assessments, with the exception of the last half-term—I know you had some difficulties then—show that he is on course to do very well in his final GCSE exams. I've read the incident report written by Mr Crawley, the Music teacher, who saw part of what happened five days ago. I've also had some input regarding Nadim's performance from all of his subject teachers as well as his form tutor. In light of everything, I can see that this incident was rather unfortunate."

"Yes, sir," Mum nodded. "Nadim is not a violent person. This is a one-off incident, which he very much regrets and will definitely never happen again."

"I completely agree, Mrs Asad," he continued, "this incident certainly doesn't reflect what we know of Nadim and I do hope it will never happen again." He then took out a paper and handed it to Mum. "This is a contract that you must sign before we allow Nadim back into the school." Mum and I read through and signed the one page 'contract', which contained some targets. I was immediately placed on a Red Behaviour Report which I had to get signed by all my subject teachers at the end of every lesson. I also had to show Ms Thomas and then get it signed by Mum when I got home every day. If all the targets were ticked for the next two weeks, then I would come off the report. Otherwise, it would be extended.

The meeting ended after the Head checked through the 'contract', which was then photocopied several times by the Head's PA. A copy was handed to Mum, one was handed to Ms Thomas and one remained in my file with the admin office. I gave Mum a tight hug and went to my lesson. I was glad that this episode was over.

"Rest assured, Mrs Asad," said the Head as we walked out, "we have dealt with ALL those who were involved in this incident and issued the appropriate sanctions."

I don't know what punishment or sanction they gave to Razor and his gang. I didn't really see them much after that. Even when I did bump into him he just seemed to avoid eye contact and always looked the other way. I didn't have any reprisals from the street boys so I assume Razor didn't tell them what happened, probably out of shame or embarrassment. I was pretty glad, because now I could keep my head down and focus on my studies.

On my journey back home, just before I turned the corner to take that long road that led into our estate, I saw Riya again. This time she was the one lost in her own world with her eyes glued to her phone and her earphones stuck in. She was walking in my direction. I waved at her several times before she actually noticed me. She looked straight up and nearly crashed into me, the force making her jerk. I nervously pulled back.

"I'm really sorry, Riya. I didn't mean to scare you."

"It's alright," she replied, her eyes still wide with surprise. "Sorry, I didn't see you there. I'm in a bit of a rush, I've got an interview at Crescent Park College this evening. Anyway, how are you?"

"I'm well, thanks. So... Crescent Park College? That's supposed to be decent." I stared into her eyes intently. I always felt mesmerised by them. She was smartly dressed in a simple long black dress and a formal jacket. Her hair was loose and untied with a few simple curls, which hung about her shoulders and bounced slightly as she talked. I could smell her hair again. A fruit flavoured shampoo or conditioner, I thought to myself as I breathed in. I cast my eyes down quickly, trying to focus on something else.

"I haven't made up my mind yet. I'm just trying to get a feel for different places before I make a final decision about where to do my A-Levels next year. I've already been to a couple of interviews but I'm still really nervous to be honest!"

"You'll be fine, Riya," I said confidently. "I'm sure you'll make the right decision. You've always been sensible."

"Aw, thanks!" She paused, a familiar little blush creeping around her cheeks. "You know, there's something different about you today," she said as she looked into my eyes searchingly, "you're not your usual doom and gloom self." She let out a small laugh, her eyes twinkling.

"I've just had a good few days, that's all," I replied, not wanting to explain my whole ordeal from the past few weeks. "Although it's been a crazy school year."

"Yeah, don't I know it! Anyway, I've got to go. Don't want to be late."

We exchanged goodbyes and I stood there watching her as she walked off into the distance. I stared for a few minutes in the direction she took. Part of me yearned to speak to her again. I wished she'd stayed for a few minutes longer. I shook my head, trying to snap out of the dreamlike state. Fear Allah, Nadim, I told myself, and walked on in the opposite direction.

* * *

It took a few weeks for the reward money to get processed. But even before it arrived, I felt overwhelmed with relief and gratefulness. I felt like life had embraced me in a much-needed hug. We didn't get Mum's gold back though. DCI Huntley told us that it went missing from their evidence room and got lost somewhere during their investigations. They chose to give Mum some compensation money instead, which she didn't mind too much since she wanted to sell the gold anyway. I thought it was a bit strange since police evidence rooms are supposed to be very secure places, but I decided not to follow it up or give it any further thought. I was just glad the whole thing was over.

The next few weeks were wonderful. The money came into my account two weeks after I was given the 'all clear' from the police. £5,000 was a lot of money and I knew I wasn't going to blow it all at once! The temptation was strong though, to spend it all and enjoy myself with it. With what I'd been through recently I felt like I needed some pampering. Plus, I didn't need to feel guilty this time. This reward money was rightfully mine and not dodgy money that I'd stumbled across. Nevertheless, I was going to be mature about it. I wanted to spend some of it on whatever I needed to, some on my family, and the rest... well, I didn't know what I wanted to do with the rest, but what I did know was that I didn't want this money to run out quickly. It was a huge blessing from Allah and I wanted it to last for as long as it could.

I started by paying off that horrid gas bill. I called the gas company and spoke to the manager. After an hour of discussions, they decided to give Mum a 50% discount on the bill since it was partly their fault that the bill was so high in the first place. No more threatening red letters that gave Mum panic attacks! I then called the gas and electricity companies to make sure that Mum was on the cheapest tariff and that she got her dual fuel discount too.

I also bought a new smart television mainly so Mum didn't get bored when we were at school. The twins loved it too. As for me, I realised how much my mind and personality developed as a result of reading so I barely had time for things like television and computer games. I did buy myself a laptop though and paid for the internet connection because that was essential to my future plans. Besides, Graham had a games console so I could always go to his house if I ever felt the urge to shoot a few zombies in Resident Evil or be a famous footballer in Fifa.

I still had a fair bit of money left so I thought about how I could invest it and make it grow so we never fell short again. I wasn't business-minded at all, but I kept on seeing these 'leave your nine to five and become rich' adverts all over social media, which forced me to do some research into setting up an online business that I could manage part-time without it interfering with my studies. I looked at things I could sell, the cost of buying them and the profit I could gain by selling them. I also looked at how much it would cost me to set up an online store and put aside some money for advertising. When I put all my ideas down onto paper, I did as much research as possible. I was surprised at how much I learned from other people's social media videos about how to set up and run a business.

I knew that students at school often forgot to bring a pen or a calculator so I decided to sell stationery, individually as well as in sets. I sold pens, pencils, scientific calculators, rubbers, rulers, protractors, folders, and a whole load of other essential things students need but sometimes forget or lose. It took some time to make the stock orders, get the delivery and set up the store, but once it was all finished I was ready to launch. I had all my logos and banners done too. I then advertised on a few social media channels and waited, armed with envelopes, labels and stamps. The stock was stored all over the flat because my bedroom was way too small to keep it all there.

I waited three days and on the fourth day, a storm of orders came through. My inbox was flooded with emails from my online platform store asking me to dispatch the orders. I worked sixteen hours a day on the first few weekends, just to keep up to speed. It got so busy that I asked Graham and Nayeem to lend a hand, which they kindly did and after the first month was over I couldn't dispatch orders anymore. I couldn't keep up. So I decided to ship all my stock to my online shop provider so they could fulfil the orders for me. It cost me a little bit more, which reduced my profits, but there was no other way.

After I got the hang of things, the whole business ran seamlessly. Customers ordered through my online store, which also collected payment. The online platform then fulfilled the order, took a cut and the rest, they transferred into my account. I monitored the whole thing from my smartphone. All I needed to do was re-stock every two months or sooner if stock started to run out.

I didn't know if this was going to work or not and I had no previous business experience. But I was a fast learner and I learnt the tricks of the trade very quickly through a lot of trial and error. The first few months were great and then things started to slow down a bit. But all I did at that time was run promotions and sales. It felt as if I threw a pebble into the dry desert and I came back three days later to find a rainforest had magically appeared! It was yet another great blessing from Allah, the Most Generous.

It brought me a steady bit of money every week. It didn't make me rich, but it certainly meant that we were going to be okay. It meant Mum didn't have to worry about living on such a tight budget where any unexpected event could throw us off course. Our current finances were like trying to cover a table with a tablecloth that was too short for it: if you covered one side, then the other end became exposed. Smart Stationery meant we could leave those days behind and focus on our futures instead of worrying about money all the time.

Chapter 22

New Horizons

It was two weeks after my sixteenth birthday. I'd already completed all my GCSE exams, having done the best I could do, and was in the middle of the longest school holidays, about eight weeks in total. I already had a conditional offer from my school's sixth form college to study A-Levels in the subjects that I loved the most: English, History, Philosophy and Business Studies.

I finally made an appointment to see my GP who told me that the stresses and strains of the last few years meant that I was suffering from anxiety and mild depression. She also said that I didn't need medication, but advised that some counselling could benefit me.

I was apprehensive about attending counselling sessions at first. I felt scared that I might actually have mental issues, and if I did, I didn't want to know. It was much easier to just bury my head in the sand and get on with life. I was also ashamed that I allowed my problems to affect me so much that I needed counselling to get me through. But I recognised that I was changing. I hadn't felt like my usual self for months and it wasn't a good change. I needed to get to grips with these sudden impulses that led me to hit Razor and hurt him quite badly. I decided that if I wanted to build myself back up again and return back to being the strong, confident and responsible person who learned from his mistakes and came out at the other end a better and improved person, then counselling was maybe the best way forward. If I wanted to deal with my internal issues, it was better to deal with them now and not leave them unresolved, because they could explode in the future with horrible consequences. I decided to listen to my doctor's advice and embrace the counselling sessions.

The sessions took place once every two weeks. I was glad I went to them because they allowed me to open up about everything I'd kept hidden for so long. Sally, my counsellor, taught me how to deal with negative emotions and how to cope with painful memories.

"When you have those memories," she said, "just fast-forward it like a DVD until you get to the 'happy' moment in that memory, because in every moment, in every memory, there will always be some positivity you can connect to. For example, when your father passed away, which was a tragic event, the part of that story of how you coped and helped your mother and siblings—those are the positive parts of that story. Just fast-forward your memory to that occasion and think positively about it."

I had ten sessions booked in total and I felt better after each one. It was soothing to have someone to offload my worries, troubles and anxieties onto, to be able to open up fully with no restraint and then work out coping mechanisms and ways to resolve unwanted feelings, emotions and anxieties. I did the mental exercises and applied Sally's advice to my life. It made me feel in control again, like I was back in the driving seat, having spent the last few weeks in the back seat with no driver.

Mum was a lot jollier and the twins, well, they were always as good as gold. As for Nabil, I sent him a bit more money every month, which allowed him to purchase phone credit from the prison and call home more often. I also sent him some clothes and new Nike Air trainers (like the ones Dad used to get for us) so he wouldn't have to wear the plain blue overalls and plimsolls that the prison issued everyone with.

For the first time in a long time, I was happy and optimistic about life. I carried positive energy with me wherever I went because I had a lot to be grateful for. I decided the focus of my business would be to serve people. That's where I found the most happiness—in being a service to people and their needs, especially people I could relate to, like students. My products were well-priced, good quality and easily accessible.

When I got the opportunity, early in the afternoon when the sun was at its peak, I took a stroll beside Regent's Canal, feeling the sun's warmth on the back of my bare neck. The canal was still, with only very small waves of tiny currents moving upwards away from the edges of the foot path. I didn't race against it. Instead, I enjoyed the soothing way the little waves ran on top of the water like a floating rubber duck, making me feel renewed and energised.

I was ambitious but I didn't plan too far ahead. For now, I just wanted to enjoy the things I already had around me: my faith, my family, my friends and my thriving online store alhamdulillah. I discovered that my happiness lay in finding contentment in my heart and not running after money. If something else comes along in this unpredictable life to change that, I will also change with it, adapt and challenge myself to find contentment again, because that's where happiness is, that's where peace is, and that's where true richness is found.

Glossary of Arabic Terms

Abaya: Arab style dress for women

Allah: Arabic name for God

Alhamdulillah: Praise be to Allah

Adhaan: Call to prayer

Astaghfirullah: Allah forgive me

Asalamu-alaykum: Islamic greeting of peace

Allahu akbar: God is Great

Amaana: A trust

Bismillah: In the name of Allah

Dhikr: Repetitive short utterances in praise of Allah

Du'a: Prayer

Dunya: Worldly life

Eid: Muslim festival

Fajr: Dawn prayer

Hijab: Islamic headscarf for women

Imam: Person leading the prayer

Isha: Night prayer

Istighfaar: Asking Allah for forgiveness

Janazah: Funeral prayer

Jummu'ah: Friday congregational prayer

Maghrib: Sunset prayer

Qur'an: Muslim Holy Book

Rakat: Unit of prayer

Ruku: Bowing in prayer

Salaam: Muslim greeting of peace

Salaah: Five compulsory daily prayers

Sujood: Prostration

Takbir: Allahu akbar

Tawakkul: Reliance upon Allah

Tawba: Asking Allah for forgiveness

Thobe: Arab style dress, similar to a long shirt

Ustaadh: Teacher

Wa-alaykum salaam: (Returning) Islamic greeting

Wallahi: Oath (By Allah)

Wudu: Ablution.

Ya: Oh

Zuhr: Prayer after midday